BENDING TO EARTH

Bending to Earth

Strange Stories by Irish Women

edited by

Maria Giakaniki
and Brian J. Showers

Swan River Press
Dublin, Ireland
MMXXI

Bending to Earth
edited by Maria Giakaniki
and Brian J. Showers

Published by
Swan River Press
Dublin, Ireland
in October MMXXI

www.swanriverpress.ie
brian@swanriverpress.ie

Cover design by Meggan Kehrli
from artwork by Karen Vaughan

Set in Garamond by Ken Mackenzie

Published with support from Dublin UNESCO
City of Literature and Dublin City Libraries.

ISBN 978-1-78380-751-2

Swan River Press published
a limited edition hardback of
Bending to Earth in March 2019.

Contents

Introduction

There is a latent urge among literary scholars to define grand traditions in literature that sweep through the centuries. Joining the dots between one author's influences on the work of another writer a generation thence makes for a tantalising and occasionally illuminating game. For some, these distinguished pedigrees are absolutely vital. Such contexts can give better understanding to the evolution of literary movements, the development of genres, and affinities between various coteries of writers.

Consider how much ink has been expended in an effort to prove whether or not Bram Stoker, author of *Dracula* (1897), had read or was definitively influenced by Joseph Sheridan Le Fanu's "Carmilla" (1871-2). Sometimes connections can be delightfully subtle, such as recognising the spine of Lord Dunsany's *The Gods of Pegāna* (1905) in a photograph of C. S. Lewis posing before a bookshelf in his study. But establishing a conscious tradition—one author knowingly working in the wake of another in an unbroken chain—can be a difficult and frequently tenuous task. This is especially true when genre is concerned, where delineations are often already nebulous.

If a novel or short story displays only scant elements of a particular school of literature, it is granted the prefix "proto"; the author, usually long dead at the time of the pronouncement, may well find herself surprised by such an inclusion. The best one can do in some cases is make an informed speculation—though the peril here is that these assertions can transform over time, without further erudition, into assumed fact.

The present volume is subtitled "Strange Stories by Irish Women", and its authors populate the better part of the nineteenth century. One might rightfully wonder if such a joined-up tradition can be delineated, and if the tales in this anthology constitute part of a literary continuum. In his essay on Irish literature for *Supernatural Literature of the World* (2005), Peter Tremayne makes a helpful observation: "Practically every Irish writer has, at some time, explored the genre for the supernatural is part of Irish culture." Indeed, one would be hard-pressed to find an Irish author who did not, at some point, include elements of the fantastic in their work—be it supernatural, folkloric, surrealist, or something else. Naturally, this makes broad declarations a particularly challenging endeavour.

What we are more certain about is that the writers included in *Bending to Earth* were not considered during their lifetimes to be chiefly writers of fantastical fiction. Yet they each at some point in their careers wandered into more speculative realms—some only briefly, others for lengthier stays. Some of them, like Katharine Tynan, Ethna Carbery, and Dora Sigerson Shorter, were known primarily as poets. Others, such as L. T. Meade and Clotilde Graves, deliberately wrote for more general popular markets; while the likes of Lady Wilde and Lady Gregory still linger in the Irish national psyche for their explorations of legends and folklore.

And then there are writers whose posthumous reputations have been sustained through the years solely on the merits of their supernatural tales, their once mainstream writings now almost entirely abandoned by modern readers. In 1882 Charlotte Riddell published her seminal collection, *Weird*

Stories, and her supernatural novellas are still celebrated for their effectiveness. Meanwhile, Riddell's realist mainstream novels have faded from memory—save for in the cloistered world of scholars and academics. Similarly, the ghostly writings of Rosa Mulholland and B. M. Croker were kept alive, with varying levels of success, by the industrious efforts of twentieth-century anthologists, while the remainder of their work passed into the afterlife of the unfashionable from which they seldom return.

In compiling this anthology of strange tales, we sought stories by Irish women writing in the broader range of the darkly fantastic. We focused on the merits of each writer and their contribution, arranging stories in a sequence that we hope makes for an agreeable read. As one might expect, these selected tales reflect the diverse backgrounds, experiences, and preoccupations of each author. While there might not be a formal pedigree in the supernatural tradition, there is certainly a more ethereal sense of connection—sometimes social, sometimes thematic—that characterises these writers and their respective offerings to strange literature.

Anna Maria Hall is primarily remembered for co-writing several volumes with her husband Samuel Carter Hall (1800-1889) based on their multiple tours of Ireland. These popular titles—including *Characteristic Sketches of Ireland* (1840), *A Week at Killarney* (1843), and *Ireland: Its Scenery and Character* (1841-3)—fuelled what was then a growing public interest in the geography, society, customs, and folklore of western Ireland. In his *Retrospect of a Long Life* (1883), Samuel Carter Hall notes that the celebrated novelist Joseph Sheridan Le Fanu and his brother William, a civic engineer, served as their "guides throughout the beautiful district around Castle Connell, and [he] found them full of anecdote and rich in antiquarian lore, with thorough knowledge of Irish peculiarities". Anna Maria Hall's fiction treads this same rural terrain. Her first short story collection, *Sketches of Irish Character* (1829), in which she often utilised memories from her childhood in Bannow, County Wexford, launched her career as a professional writer.

For this anthology we chose Hall's "The Dark Lady", originally published in *The Drawing-Room Table-Book: An Annual for Christmas and the New Year* (1847). Unsurprisingly, given its inclusion in a Christmas annual, "The Dark Lady" is a ghost story in keeping with the yuletide tradition. Although Hall wrote mainly about her native country, this particular tale is not set in Ireland; the plot instead unfolds in the Swiss Alps. This continental setting and the main motifs that accompany it—the isolated castle, the motherless maiden, the young female friend, and the ruined family chapel in which an ancestral apparition dwells—anticipate Le Fanu's vampire novella "Carmilla".

Endowed with qualities endemic to the familiar heroine of the high-gothic novel—beauty, virtue, and defiance of a patriarchal guardian's strict authority—the young Amelie de Rohean proves fearless when confronting the eerie world of the spirits: she regularly visits the haunted family chapel alone at night where she converses with a disembodied entity. This spectral tale deftly combines the gothic romances of the late eighteenth century with Victorian supernaturalism. Moreover, and as a reflection, perhaps, of Hall's lifelong interests in both spiritualism and women's rights, "The Dark Lady" contains a distinctly feminist subtext throughout: the benevolent female spirit, a forceful opposition to decidedly masculine expressions of egocentricity, cruelty, and emotional detachment are among the story's most important themes.

By contrast, the next tale features an isolated Irish setting, even though to the contemporary reader it might have seemed as equally remote as Hall's faraway Switzerland. Lady Wilde's "The Child's Dream" takes us to *Inis Airc*—Shark Island—a barren and now uninhabited isle off the coast of County Galway. During the late nineteenth century, this outpost in the Atlantic still sustained a small community, complete with local stories and superstitions. Like many writers of their generation, such as T. Crofton Croker or William Carleton, both Lady Wilde and Sir William Wilde (1815-1876) were driven by a revived interest in "the fairy-haunted hills and lakes and raths of ancient Ireland", and set about collecting traditions and legends of "the old race" for their urban audience. Drawing on some of the same material Sir William used for his *Irish Popular Superstitions* (1852), Lady Wilde composed her two-volume *Ancient Legends, Mystic Charms and Superstitions of Ireland* (1887), which interweaves folklore with retellings of local legends.

"The Child's Dream" is one of many tales in *Legends, Charms and Superstitions* set on Shark Island. In the preface to this work, Lady Wilde is dismissive of superstition, claiming that these beliefs were products of an ignorant and uncultivated peasantry—ironically the very people from whom she derives her stories. She also refers to the blending of "pagan myths and the Christian legend" in the oral traditions of these rural people. And yet "The Child's Dream" stands as a lyrical narrative that brings to mind the melancholy fairy tales written by her son, Oscar, such as "The Selfish Giant" and "The Happy Prince", in which poetic fantasy mingles with Christian imagery. But Lady Wilde's story is far less ornate. Stylistically, her writing is heavily indebted to the oral folk tradition. As such, her work rejects the baroque literariness and textual intricacies employed by her son. Whether "The Child's Dream" is read as oral folklore corrupted by the telling or as fiction filtered through writerly artifice, Lady Wilde expresses a genuine "love for the beautiful island" that offered her "first inspiration".

Several years later, and working in a similar vein as Wilde, Lady Gregory continued the practise of collecting and writing down oral folklore, making her own attempts at exploring and understanding the origins of Irish national identity. Her retellings of Irish mythologies in *Cuchulain of Muirthemne* (1902) and *Gods and Fighting Men* (1904) are considered touchstones of the Celtic Revival, and remain in print to this day. Lady Gregory began collecting "news from the invisible world" for her *Visions and Beliefs in the West of Ireland* (1920) on the heels of reading W. B. Yeats's *The Celtic Twilight* (1893), and subsequently meeting that book's author. Whereas Yeats often focused on Sligo, Lady Gregory explains in her preface that she "felt jealous for Galway", and so concentrated her own efforts on that part of the country.

"The Unquiet Dead", an extract from *Visions and Beliefs*, is comprised of several fragments told by those who have glimpsed the world of the unseen. These brief tales take the form of first person reports concerning ghostly appearances and spectral encounters, giving each narration a certain sense of immediacy. "Even when I began to gather these stories," notes Lady Gregory, "I cared less for the evidence given in them than for the beautiful rhythmic sentences in which they were told." And yet she clearly shows sympathy for belief in the "invisible world", and dutifully records each encounter with little authorial imposition. This close connection between the uncanny and our earthly world—the easy fluidity between the domains of life and death—renders these supernatural manifestations almost ordinary, as if they are within the realm of natural experience. Unlike the other works presented in this anthology, "The Unquiet Dead" is not built on the more familiar structure of the short story. Instead, the presentation of these eerie folk-narratives in the manner of first-hand testimonies gives them a vividness which more than qualifies them for inclusion here.

Next comes L. T. Meade's "The Woman with the Hood", which, like Anna Maria Hall's "The Dark Lady", was published for the Christmas season—albeit fifty years later. Meade is very likely Ireland's most prolific writer. Some bibliographers number her output at over three hundred titles—not including those on which she collaborated with various co-writers. At the peak of her career she was producing a staggering ten books per year, which garnered a legion of loyal readers. While much of her writing has fallen into obscurity, some of her books are still enjoyed today, such as *The Brotherhood of the Seven Kings* (1899) and *The Sorceress of the Strand* (1903), both of which feature female villains. Part of Meade's dizzying success was her ability to write across a range of commercial genres—often aimed at adolescent girls—including school stories, mysteries (such as those of the detective Miss Cusack), adventures, and, of course, tales of the macabre and ghostly.

Meade's story centres on Miss Frayling, of Garth Hall, a wealthy young woman who is mercilessly haunted by the strange apparition of the title. In an interesting twist, the spirit does not appear to the narrator, Doctor Bruce, who is called upon to treat Miss Frayling. Instead, he perceives the phantom only as a disembodied voice that calls to him in the night, pleading for him to return to the Hall. Meade's prompt and tidy ending elicits an even greater sense of the macabre for the questions that remain unanswered. While we may learn the basis for the haunting, we are still in the dark as to what nefarious event first caused the Woman with the Hood to chill the corridors of Garth Hall. Published in the Christmas number of the *Weekly Scotsman* (1897), "The Woman with the Hood" is a prime example of a *fin de siècle* spectral yarn.

For the following tale, we return to rural Ireland, this time to a lonely thatch-roofed cottage in the northern county of Antrim. Although the nationalist poet Ethna Carbery is not usually associated with literature of the strange and supernatural, like most Irish authors, her writing makes the occasional foray into the Land Beyond. In a memoir of his late wife, Seumus MacManus wrote, "The unseen world was always close to her, and its gates for her were always ajar, giving her frequent glimpses of the land of beauty and wonder." "The Wee Gray Woman"—from the posthumous volume *The Passionate Hearts* (1903)—is one of these glimpses.

Carbery's descriptive prose has a strong poetic sensibility, and a lyrical melancholy saturates every sentence of this tale. Having spent her childhood in Ballymena, Carbery was familiar with the slow-creeping mists that could rise from bogs surrounding the nearby parish of Glenwherry, where the tale is set. The way in which Carbery evokes the rural community and landscape with distinct realism paradoxically suggests the perpetual threat of the otherworldly, much in the same way eye-witnesses matter-of-factly report similar such intrusions in "The Unquiet Dead".

Readers will note that "The Wee Gray Woman" is a decidedly gentler if not sadder tale, and the ghost here is neither malign nor vengeful. Instead, the supernatural element is peripheral and ambiguous, and the mysterious hearth-side visitor of the story's title would seem to serve as a haunting reminder of some past tragedy that played out on the wild bog many years ago. The Wee Gray Woman is a symbol of unresolved misery but, unexpectedly, a comforting one.

Ethna Carbery's gifted career came to a sad end when she died at the age of thirty-five, less than a year after marrying MacManus. He writes: "And thus, when she was elatedly congratulating herself that her work for Ireland was begun in earnest, she suddenly found the Noiseless One, leaning over her shoulder, take the pen from her eager hand and across the well-begun page write—Finis."

Beatrice Grimshaw is less connected with Ireland than she is with the South Seas—and for good reason. In an essay entitled "How I Found Adventure" (1939), Grimshaw wrote that she was born in a "big lonely country house" five miles from Belfast. But she would not remain there for long. She continues: "There were maps of far-away places, maps with tantalising blanks in them; maps of the huge Pacific, coloured an entrancing blue. I swore that I would go there." This she did. Commissioned by a London newspaper to write travel articles, she booked passage to the South Seas where she spent much of the rest of her life exploring Java, the New Hebrides, the Solomon Islands, New Guinea, and beyond—terrain still then unknown to European tourists. Writing about Ireland and typical Irish themes must have been far from Grimshaw's mind. Instead she penned travelogues with sensational titles such as *From Fiji to the Cannibal Islands* (1907) and *In the Strange South Seas* (1908). "I managed to make friends with the wild men of the woods," she reminisced. "I came in contact with the amazing native magic of the sorcerer, and lived in a house that was haunted by ghostly birds . . . . I was present at a dance of murderers and man-eaters, up in the Tanna hills, where no man went." Her autobiography, *Isles of Adventure* (1930), details a truly determined and extraordinary life.

Grimshaw's "The Blanket Fiend" (1929) is perhaps the most incongruous story we have chosen for this volume. There are neither traditional ghosts nor gothic ruins, and the supernatural is traded for the preternatural. "The Blanket Fiend" has more in common with the colonial adventures of H. Rider Haggard than the ghost stories of M. R. James, with perhaps a slight, albeit superficial, flavour of H. P. Lovecraft. The plot unfolds in New Guinea with its strange jungle landscape replete with an isolated tribe, superstitious beliefs, ritual dances, and sacrifices to a primordial presence older than the jungle itself.

Regretfully, what Grimshaw has more in common with Lovecraft is racism and misogyny. Readers will note that such attitudes are present not just in "The Blanket Fiend", but in other examples of Grimshaw's work. However, we have chosen to leave the text intact, as it was written. Despite the objectionable elements, the tale is a compelling one, showing, we hope, the range of theme in strange literature, while acknowledging that not all recovered voices share our present attitudes.

Like many of her generation, Katharine Tynan's legacy is now a footnote in the national narrative of W. B. Yeats—a domineering force that asserts its influence over all Irish literature. Tynan spent her early years at Whitehall, the family home in Clondalkin. Here she hosted a popular salon that attracted the luminaries of the Irish Literary Renaissance: not only young Willie Yeats, but also Lady Gregory, George William Russell (A.E.), Ethna Carbery, and Dora Sigerson Shorter. Her broader circle also included Lady Wilde and Lord Dunsany. Tynan's first publications were poems in the *Irish Monthly*, though soon she started writing prose at the suggestion of Rosa Mulholland. Tynan fondly recalled her mentor in her memoir *Twenty-Five Years* (1913): "I worshipped [Mulholland] whole-heartedly . . . . I have had few things in my life more exquisite than those afternoons I used to spend with her." Over the course of her lengthy career, Tynan also contributed to *Atalanta*, a magazine for girls, which was at the time edited by L. T. Meade; and to the nationalist monthly *Bean na hÉireann* (*The Women of Ireland*), noted for its strong feminist leanings.

One of Tynan's earliest collections, *An Isle in the Water* (1895), features stories set on a fictitious island off the west coast of Ireland. "I was brought up on the dreadful churchyard stories of the Irish peasant imagination," she notes in her memoir. Sure enough, *An Isle in the Water* contains a handful of forays into the ghostly realm, including "The First Wife". As the title suggests, this story of domestic spectrality uses the supernatural to explore the relationship between a dead woman, her former domain, and her husband's new wife. Other authors such as Edith Wharton and May Sinclair employed this same motif in which a dead wife witnesses a new domestic life that she cannot participate in, inevitably pitting herself against the interloper. However, unlike Wharton and Sinclair, Tynan emphasises the passing of identity, loss of agency, and an inevitable resignation that culminates in a particularly heart-breaking ending. Tynan's prose is elegant, and like Ethna Carbery, she exhibits an assured sense of poetic language in her fable-like storytelling.

The Sigerson household on Clare Street, like Tynan's Clondalkin salon, was another intellectual hub for Victorian Dublin's artists and politicians. Hester Sigerson (1828-1898) contributed poetry and stories to several Dublin magazines such as *Young Ireland, Irish Fireside*, and *Irish Monthly*; while her husband, George Sigerson (1836-1925), was a prominent neurologist, poet, politician, and Gaelic scholar. So too did their daughters, Hetty and Dora, display much talent: "We were all possessed with the common impulse towards literature," wrote Tynan of this period. "We were all making our poems and stories. Dora Sigerson, who was then a strikingly handsome girl, was painting as well, making statuettes and busts, doing all sorts of things, and looking like a young Muse."

As a passionate nationalist and leading light of the Irish Revival, Dora Sigerson Shorter became not only an accomplished poet, but also a political activist, heading an unsuccessful campaign to prevent the execution of the

Irish revolutionary Roger Casement, who had been found guilty of high treason. Shorter's posthumous collection of verse *Sixteen Dead Men and Other Poems of Easter Week* (1919) serves as a tribute to the Easter Rising of 1916—and another memorial to the Rising, this one sculpted by Shorter in marble, still stands in Dublin's Glasnevin cemetery, near to where she is now buried. Shorter's work was championed not only by her friend Katharine Tynan, who penned a short memoir for Shorter's *The Sad Years* (1918), but also by Thomas Hardy, who wrote a prefatory note for her posthumous volume *A Dull Day in London and Other Sketches* (1920).

The Father Confessor: Stories of Death and Danger (1900) was Shorter's first collection, and features a number of unsettling tales, including "Transmigration". This gloomy tale about a spirit-exchange between two living men is an odyssey of corruption and sin. The doppelgänger motif—in particular committing crimes in the guise of another—has deep roots in decadent literature exemplified by novels such as *The Private Memoirs and Confessions of a Justified Sinner* (1824) by James Hogg and Stevenson's *Strange Case of Dr. Jekyll and Mr. Hyde* (1886). Readers will also note thematic affinities with *The Picture of Dorian Gray* (1890) by Shorter's fellow countryman Oscar Wilde. "Transmigration" is a nightmare told from the villain's point of view, allowing Shorter to explore the notion of evil more explicitly. While there are hints of demonic possession, there is also room for psychological interpretations, such as paranoia or split personality. Shorter's story of soul transference is disturbing, quite possibly the most jarring in this volume.

Leaving the lurid urban setting of "Transmigration", we return to the west of Ireland with "Not to Be Taken at Bed-Time", a tale of rural witchcraft written for the Christmas magazine market of 1865. The Belfast-born

Rosa Mulholland, later Lady Gilbert, enjoyed a lengthy and prosperous career: she published a two-volume biography of her husband—the historian Sir John T. Gilbert (1829-1898)—poetry, novels for young girls, and short stories, often with a strong Catholic bent. Early in her career Mulholland drew the attention of Charles Dickens, who published her work in *Household Words*, as well as many of her ghost stories in the Christmas numbers of *All the Year Round*, including the story we have selected for this anthology. Later Mulholland became associated with Fr. Matthew Russell's popular magazine *Irish Monthly*, both as contributor and editor. In this capacity she helped foster a new generation of Irish writers. Among the publication's contributors were Dora Sigerson Shorter, Oscar Wilde, and Katharine Tynan.

Mulholland penned a number of strange tales over the years. While a handful of these were collected in *The Haunted Organist of Hurley Burley* (1891), it was not until 2013 that editor Richard Dalby assembled an expanded selection of Mulholland's most notable offerings. "Not to Be Taken at Bed-Time" is possibly Mulholland's best known story, being for a time heavily anthologised after its appearance in Montague Summers's landmark volume *The Supernatural Omnibus* (1931).

Like much of Mulholland's writing, such as *The Wicked Woods of Tobereevil* (1872) and *Banshee Castle* (1895), "Not to Be Taken at Bed-Time" features a rural Irish setting and incorporates elements of folklore with flourishes of the supernatural. This grim tale of dark sorcery and unrequited love takes place in the picturesque region of Connemara in County Galway. The story's archetypal witch is a "yellow-faced hag" named Pexie na Pishrogie—*pishogue* being Irish for superstition or charm. With her "elf-locks of coarse black hair" and smattering of Gaelic phraseology,

Mulholland simultaneously evokes, albeit in caricature, the world of faerie and that of the Irish-speaking peasantry. With further narrative notes that are reminiscent of the Brothers Grimm, in particular "Snow White", Mulholland delivers a European faerie tale wholly populated with Irish settings and characters.

Similar to some of the other writers in this volume, B. M. Croker wrote numerous strange stories for the magazine market, later mixing them with non-fantastical tales in her collections, such as *The Old Cantonment* (1905) and *Odds and Ends* (1919). As Richard Dalby had done for Rosa Mulholland, he also gathered Croker's genre work for publication as a single volume: *"Number Ninety" and Other Ghost Stories* (2000). However, unlike the other writers, Croker's stories were not anthologised quite as often, and so her strange tales languished until the latter part of the twentieth century. Yet throughout her career Croker was an immensely popular and best-selling author—with one odd exception. In a letter to her publisher, Edmund Downey, Croker notes, "It is strange to me that I never receive any acknowledgement from my native land as an Irish novelist . . . Irish papers rarely notice me, save *The Freeman's Journal*, whose abuse is most amusing."

Croker was indeed Irish, having been born in Kilgefin, County Roscommon, but like Beatrice Grimshaw, her fictions were generally set much further afield. In 1870 she married Lt.-Col. John Stokes Croker, then of the 21st Royal Scots Fusiliers. Shortly thereafter she accompanied him to India and Southeast Asia, where they lived for several years: Madras, Bengal, and later a hill-station in Wellington; then on to Burma and the Andaman Islands. It was in India, as Croker explains in an 1896 interview, that she "secretly drew out her pen" in an effort to "amuse herself and to beguile the long, weary days". Often reflective of her own experiences, Croker's romances are drawn largely from the daily life of colonial India, a setting that would have communicated a sense of exoticism to her contemporary readers. The Crokers eventually retired to Bray, County Wicklow, where their house, Lordello, was "liberally decorated with tiger and leopard skins, Indian daggers, knives, horns and other trophies, whilst a magnificent stuffed tiger's head with gnashing teeth hangs over a door facing the entrance".

Much as India held sway over Croker's writing, she also wrote a number of novels and stories set in her native Ireland. "The Red Woollen Necktie" from *In the Kingdom of Kerry* (1886), is one such tale. Croker begins the story by invoking Lord Byron's apocalyptic poem "Darkness" (1816)—"*I had a dream which was not all a dream*"—summoning a note of bleak eventuality. The story features a premonitory daydream followed by a frightening occurrence made all the more alarming for its doom-laden sense of *déjà vu*. Croker uses this tale of psychical terror to create a sympathetic protagonist—a young woman in an isolated country house, threatened by "a dark shadow . . . a tall, powerful man". Rebuked by her father and brother, she is forced to rely on her own intuition as she faces an uncertain future.

Of all the authors represented in this volume, Charlotte Riddell is probably most recognised as a stalwart veteran of the ghost story genre. She ranks alongside Joseph Sheridan Le Fanu for her craftsmanship and ability to evoke the supernatural. Riddell started her career as a professional writer at an early age. Her father died while she was still young—he had been the sheriff for County Antrim—and the family subsequently fell into hardship. Out of necessity, Riddell helped supplement the family income with her pen. She moved to London in 1855, and two years later married a stove and boiler merchant named Joseph Hadley Riddell. She commenced writing a steady stream of novels, many under the name "Mrs. J. H. Riddell", by which she is still sometimes known. By 1867 Riddell became the editor and part-proprietor of *St. James's Magazine*, which had been founded by Anna Maria Hall a few years earlier. Most of Riddell's novels, such as *George Geith, of Fen Court* (1864) and *The Head of the Firm* (1892), consider as their themes the social and financial struggles of urban life—a plight that resonated with many of her readers. Her ghost stories frequently exploit similar anxieties, featuring secret wills, lost fortunes, and unexpected inheritances.

Spectral tales constitute a major part of Riddell's work. Her collection *Weird Stories* (1882), a favourite among connoisseurs, is frequently reprinted and usually augmented with further tales. Riddell wrote in the region of twenty ghost stories, including four novellas in which the supernatural features prominently—and there may well be more stories tucked away in crumbling pages of forgotten magazines. Tales like "The Banshee's Warning" (1867) and "The Old House on Vauxhall Walk" (1882) are still capable of delivering a pleasing terror to today's readers.

"The De Grabrooke Monument" is perhaps aesthetically closer to eighteenth-century gothic romances than are most of Riddell's more Victorian narratives, which usually feature haunted houses or mansions. Instead, this lengthy tale is distinguished by its overtly gothic trappings: a doomed romance, a family murder, and ancestral ghosts. The set-up is classic: a young woman becomes accidentally trapped overnight in an ancient, ruined cathedral . . . the perfect setting for Charlotte Riddell to unleash her long, creeping shadows. "The De Grabrooke Monument" is a previously unknown ghost story by Riddell. It was originally published in *Routledge's Every Girl's Annual 1879*, and we are particularly pleased to reprint it here for the first time in 140 years.

Our final story is a *conte cruel* from the shadowy realm; a one-act tale with two principal players: one man and one woman. "A Vanished Hand" (1914) was written by "Richard Dehan"—the pen name of the dramatist and novelist Clotilde Graves. Born in County Cork, Graves studied at the Royal Female School of Art in Bloomsbury. She spent her early years in the theatre, both as an actor and as a playwright—at one point co-adapting H. Rider Haggard's popular novel *She* for the stage. Graves led a life considered at the time to be unconventional—the epitome of the "New Woman". According to an obituary in the *New Zealand Evening Post* (January 1933), "[Graves] wore short hair and affected a masculine manner and cut of costume and smoked cigarettes in public some thirty-five years ago, when such characteristics were considered eccentric." This fluidity of gender continued throughout her life. For her first novel, *Dragon's Teeth* (1891), Graves adopted the *nom de plume* "Richard Dehan", ostensibly to differentiate her theatre work from her career as a novelist. Her most famous novel, *The Dop Doctor* (1910), set against the backdrop of the Boer War, went through some thirty editions—and was adapted as a film in 1915. For as popular as she once was, Graves is seldom read today. As contemporary critic Grant Overton observed, perhaps with more prescience than he was aware, "There was once a time when there was no Richard Dehan. There now are times when there is no Clotilde Graves."

"A Vanished Hand", published in *The Cost of Wings and Other Stories* (1914), is a tale of vanity and the illusion of romantic love. The scene opens on an echo of the decadent Eighteen-Nineties: a plush London studio illuminated by the last rays of a smoky-red sunset. The room's sole occupant is a self-indulgent artist whose talent thrives on the anguished memory of his lost love, now some fifteen years in the grave. As he works on his manuscript—idealising in memory his "whole-souled, high-hearted woman"—there comes a proverbial knock at the door. Graves builds her narrative with a certain sense of macabre glee; comparisons with W. W. Jacobs's "The Monkey's Paw" (1902) would not be amiss. And while this is decidedly a tale from beyond the grave, the uncanny element deftly serves Graves's intended emotional impact. "A Vanished Hand" is effectively a devastating twist on the Orpheus myth, and the perfect way to end this volume.

These twelve strange stories by Irish women are our choices, and represent only a small selection from a much broader range of possibilities. Certainly many names, both past and present, are missing from these pages. No doubt in the hands of other editors, the contents of this book might have taken on a vastly different shape. One could explore the gothic romances of Regina Maria Roche and Maria Edgeworth; so too could selections from Dorothy Macardle's *Earth-Bound* (1924) be considered, or any number of the masterful uncanny tales by Elizabeth Bowen—not to mention a host of authors now wholly forgotten. In any case, we hope *Bending to Earth* stands as an invitation to the curious; that these strange stories of ghosts and witches, of cryptids and madmen, will serve as a lighted candle for those who wish to further illuminate the darker corners of Irish literature.

Maria Giakaniki
and Brian J. Showers
7 February 2019

Bending to Earth

The Dark Lady

Anna Maria Hall

People find it easy enough to laugh at "spirit-stories" in broad daylight, when the sunbeams dance upon the grass, and the deepest forest glades are spotted and checkered only by the tender shadows of leafy trees; when the rugged castle, that looked so mysterious and so stern in the looming night, seems suited for a lady's bower; when the rushing waterfall sparkles in diamond showers, and the hum of bee and song of bird tune the thoughts to hopes of life and happiness; people may laugh at ghosts then, if they like, but as for me, I never could merely smile at the records of those shadowy visitors. I have large faith in things supernatural, and cannot disbelieve solely on the ground that I lack such evidences as are supplied by the senses; for they, in truth, sustain by palpable proofs so few of the many marvels by which we are surrounded, that I would rather reject them altogether as witnesses, than abide the issue entirely as they suggest.

My great grandmother was a native of the canton of Berne; and at the advanced age of ninety, her memory of "the long ago" was as active as it could have been at fifteen: she looked as if she had just stepped out of a piece of tapestry belonging to a past age, but with warm sympathies for the present. Her English, when she became excited, was very curious—a mingling of French, certainly not Parisian, with here and there scraps of German done into English, literally—so that her observations were at times remarkable for their strength. "The mountains," she would say, "in her country, went high, high up, until they could look into the heavens, and *hear* God in the storm." She never thoroughly comprehended the real beauty of England, but spoke with contempt of the flatness of our island—calling our mountains "inequalities", nothing more—holding our agriculture "cheap", saying that the land tilled itself, leaving man nothing to do. She would sing the most amusing *patois* songs, and tell stories from morning till night, more especially spirit-stories: but the old lady would not tell a tale of that character a second time to an unbeliever; such things, she would say, "are not for make-laugh". One in particular, I remember, always excited great interest in her young listeners, from its mingling of the real and the romantic; but it can never be told as she told it: there was so much of the picturesque about the old lady—so much to admire in the curious carving of her ebony cane, in the beauty of her point lace, the size and weight of her long ugly earrings, the fashion of her solid silk gown, the singularity of her buckled shoes—her dark-brown wrinkled face, every wrinkle an expression—her broad thoughtful brow, beneath which glittered her bright blue eyes—bright, even when her eyelashes were white with years. All these peculiarities gave impressive effect to her words.

"In my young time," she told us, "I spent many happy hours with Amelie de Rohean, in her uncle's castle. He was a fine man—much size, stern, and dark, and full of noise—a strong man, no fear—he had a great heart, and a big head.

"The castle was situated in the midst of the most stupendous Alpine scenery, and yet it was not solitary. There were other dwellings in sight; some very near, but separated by a ravine, through which, at all seasons, a rapid river kept its foaming course. You do not know what torrents are in this country; your torrents are as babies—ours are giants. The one I speak of divided the valley; here and there a rock, round which it sported, or stormed, according to the season. In two of the defiles these rocks were of great value; acting as piers for the support of bridges—the only means of communication with our opposite neighbours.

" 'Monsieur', as we always called the count, was, as I have told you, a dark, stern, violent man. All men are wilful, my dear young ladies," she would say; "but Monsieur was the most wilful: all men are selfish; but he was the most selfish: all men are tyrants—" Here the old lady was invariably interrupted by her relatives, with "Oh, good Granny!" and, "Oh, fie, dear Granny!" and she would bridle up a little and fan herself; then continue—"Yes, my dears, each creature according to its nature—all men are tyrants; and I confess that I do think a Swiss, whose mountain inheritance is nearly coeval with the creation of the mountains, has a *right* to be tyrannical; I did not intend to blame him for that: I did not, because I had grown used to it. Amelie and I always stood up when he entered the room, and never sat down until we were desired. He never bestowed a loving word or a kind look upon either of us. We never spoke except when we were spoken to."

"But when you and Amelie were alone, dear Granny?"

"Oh, why, then we did chatter, I suppose; though then it was in moderation: for Monsieur's influence chilled us even when he was not present; and often she would say, 'It is hard trying to love him, for he will not let me!' There is no such beauty in the world now as Amelie's. I can see her as she used to stand before the richly carved glass in the grave oak-pannelled dressing-room; her luxuriant hair combed up from her full round brow; the discreet maidenly cap, covering the back of her head; her brocaded silk, (which she had inherited from her grandmother), shaded round the bosom by the modest ruffle; her black velvet gorget and bracelets, showing off to perfection the pearly transparency of her skin. She was the loveliest of all creatures, and as good as she was lovely; it seems but as yesterday that we were together—but as yesterday! And yet I lived to see her an old woman; so they called her, but she never seemed old to me! My own dear Amelie!" Ninety years had not dried up the sources of poor Granny's tears, nor chilled her heart; and she never spoke of Amelie without emotion. "Monsieur was very proud of his niece, because she was part of himself: she added to his consequence, she contributed to his enjoyment; she had grown necessary; she was the one sunbeam of his house."

"Not the *one* sunbeam, surely, Granny!" one of us would exclaim; "you were a sunbeam then."

"I was nothing where Amelie was—nothing but her shadow! The bravest and best in the country would have rejoiced to be to her what I was—her chosen friend; and some would have periled their lives for one of the sweet smiles which played around her uncle, but never touched his heart. Monsieur never would suffer people to be happy except in his way. He had never married; and he declared Amelie never should. She had, he said, as much enjoyment as he had: she had a castle with a drawbridge; she had a forest for hunting; dogs and horses; servants and serfs; jewels, gold, and gorgeous dresses; a guitar and a harpsichord; a parrot— and a friend! And such an uncle! he believed there was not such another uncle in broad Europe! For many a long day Amelie laughed at this catalogue of advantages—that is, she laughed when her uncle left the room—she never laughed before him. In time, the laugh came not; but in its place, sighs and tears. Monsieur had a great deal to answer for. Amelie was not prevented from seeing the gentry when they came to visit in a formal way, and she met many hawking and hunting; but she never was permitted to invite any one to the castle, nor to accept an invitation. Monsieur fancied that by shutting her lips, he closed her heart; and boasted such was the advantage of his good training, that Amelie's mind was fortified against all weaknesses, for she had not the least dread of wandering about the ruined chapel of the castle, where he himself dared not go after dusk. This place was dedicated to the family ghost—the spirit, which for many years had it entirely at its own disposal. It was much attached to its quarters, seldom leaving them, except for the purpose of interfering when anything decidedly wrong was going forward in the castle. 'La Femme Noir' had been seen gliding along the unprotected parapet of the bridge, and standing on a pinnacle, before the late master's death; and many tales were told of her, which in this age of unbelief would not be credited."

"Granny, did you know why your friend ventured so fearlessly into the ghost's territories?" inquired my cousin.

"I am not come to that," was the reply; "and you are one saucy little maid to ask what I do not choose to tell. Amelie certainly entertained no fear of the spirit; 'La Femme Noir' could have had no angry feelings towards her, for my friend would wander in the ruins, taking no note of daylight, or moonlight, or even darkness. The peasants declared their young lady must have walked over crossed bones, or drank water out of a raven's skull, or passed nine times round the spectre's glass on Midsummer Eve. She must have done all this, if not more: there could be little doubt that the 'Femme Noir' had initiated her into certain mysteries; for they heard at times voices in low, whispering converse, and saw the shadows of two persons cross the old roofless chapel, when 'Mamselle' had passed the foot-bridge alone. Monsieur gloried in this fearlessness on the part of his gentle niece; and more than once, when he had revellers in the castle, he sent her forth at midnight to bring him a bough from a tree that only grew beside the altar of the old chapel; and she did his bidding always as willingly, though not as rapidly, as he could desire.

"But certainly Amelie's courage brought no calmness. She became pale; her pillow was often moistened by her tears; her music was neglected; she took no pleasure in the chase; and her chamois not receiving its usual attention, went off into the mountains. She avoided me—her friend! who would have died for her; she left me alone; she made no reply to my prayers, and did not heed my entreaties. One morning, when her eyes were fixed upon a book she did not read, and I sat at my embroidery a little apart, watching the tears stray over her cheek, until I was blinded by my own, I heard Monsieur's heavy tramp approaching through the long gallery; some boots creak—but the boots of Monsieur!—they growled!"

" 'Save me, oh save me!' she exclaimed wildly. Before I could reply, her uncle banged open the door, and stood before us like an embodied thunderbolt. He held an open letter in his hand—his eyes glared—his nostrils were distended—he trembled so with rage, that the cabinets and old china shook again.

" 'Do you,' he said, 'know Charles le Maître?

"Amelie replied, 'She did.'

" 'How did you make acquaintance with the son of my deadliest foe?'

"There was no answer. The question was repeated. Amelie said she had met him, and at last confessed it was in the ruined portion of the castle! She threw herself at her uncle's feet—she clung to his knees: love taught her eloquence. She told him how deeply Charles regretted the long-standing feud; how earnest, and true, and good he was. Bending low, until her tresses were heaped upon the floor, she confessed, modestly, but firmly, that she loved this young man; that she would rather sacrifice the wealth of the whole world than forget him.

"Monsieur seemed suffocating; he tore off his lace cravat, and scattered its fragments on the floor—still she clung to him. At last he flung her from him; he reproached her with the bread she had eaten, and heaped odium upon her mother's memory! But though Amelie's nature was tender and affectionate, the old spirit of the old race roused within her; the slight girl arose, and stood erect before the man of storms.

" 'Did you think,' she said, 'because I bent to you that I am feeble? because I bore with you, have I no thoughts? You gave food to this frame, but you fed not my heart; you gave me nor love, nor tenderness, nor sympathy; you showed me to your friends, as you would your horse. If you had by kindness sown the seeds of love within my bosom; if you had been a father to me in tenderness, I would have been to you—a child. I never knew the time when I did not tremble at your footstep; but I will do so no more. I would gladly have loved you, trusted you, cherished you; but I feared to let you know I had a heart, lest you should tear and insult it. Oh, sir, those who expect love where they give none, and confidence where there is no trust, blast the fair time of youth, and lay up for themselves an unhonoured old age.' The scene terminated by Monsieur's falling down in a fit, and Amelie's being conveyed fainting to her chamber.

"That night the castle was enveloped by storms; they came from all points of the compass—thunder, lightning, hail, and rain! The master lay in his stately bed and was troubled; he could hardly believe that Amelie spoke the words he had heard: cold-hearted and selfish as he was, he was also a clear-seeing man, and it was their truth that struck him. But still his heart was hardened; he had commanded Amelie to be locked into her chamber, and her lover seized and imprisoned when he came to his usual tryst. Monsieur, I have said, lay in his stately bed, the lightning, at intervals, illumining his dark chamber. I had cast myself on the floor outside her door, but could not hear her weep, though I knew that she was overcome of sorrow. As I sat, my head resting against the lintel of the door, a form passed through the solid oak from her chamber, without the bolts being withdrawn. I saw it, as plainly as I see your faces now, under the influence of various emotions; nothing opened, but it passed through—a shadowy form, dark and vapoury, but perfectly distinct. I knew it was 'La Femme Noir', and I trembled, for she never came from caprice, but always for a purpose. I did not fear for Amelie, for 'La Femme Noir' never warred with the high-minded or virtuous. She passed slowly, more slowly than I am speaking, along the corridor, growing taller and taller as she went on, until she entered Monsieur's chamber by the door, exactly opposite where I stood. She paused at the foot of the plumed bed, and the lightning, no longer fitful, by its broad flashes kept up a perpetual illumination. She stood for some time perfectly motionless, though in a loud tone the master demanded whence she came, and what she wanted. At last, during a pause in the storm, she told him that all the power he possessed should not prevent the union of Amelie and Charles. I heard her voice myself; it sounded like the night wind among fir-trees—cold and shrill, chilling both ear and heart. I turned my eyes away while she spoke, and when I looked again, she was gone! The storm continued to increase in violence, and the master's rage kept pace with the war of elements. The servants were trembling with undefined terror; they feared they knew not what: the dogs added to their apprehension by howling fearfully, and then barking in the highest possible key: the master paced about his chamber, calling in vain on his domestics, stamping and swearing like a maniac. At last, amid flashes of lightning, he made his way to the head of the great staircase, and presently the clang of the alarum-bell mingled with the thunder and the roar of the mountain torrents: this hastened the servants to his presence, though they seemed hardly capable of understanding his words. He insisted on Charles being brought before him. We all trembled, for he was mad and livid with rage. The warden, in whose care the young man was, dared not enter the hall that echoed his loud words and heavy footsteps, for when he went to seek his prisoner, he found every bolt and bar withdrawn, and the iron door wide open;—he was gone! Monsieur seemed to find relief by his energies being called into action; he ordered instant pursuit, and mounted his favourite charger, despite the storm, despite the fury of the elements. Although the great gates rocked, and the castle shook like an aspen-leaf, he set forth, his path illumined by the lightning. Bold and brave as was his horse, he found it almost impossible to get it forward: he dug his spurs deep into the flanks of the noble animal, until the red blood mingled with the rain. At last it rushed madly down the path to the bridge the young man must cross; and when they reached it, the master discerned the floating cloak of the pursued a few yards in advance. Again the horse rebelled against his will, the lightning flashed in his eyes, and the torrent seemed a mass of red fire: no sound could be heard but of its roaring waters: the attendants clung as they advanced to the hand-rail of the bridge. The youth, unconscious of the *pursuit*, proceeded rapidly; and again roused, the horse plunged forward. On the instant, the form of 'La Femme Noir' passed with the blast that rushed down the ravine; the torrent followed in her track, and more than half the bridge was swept away forever. As the master reined back the horse he had so urged forward, he saw the youth kneeling with outstretched arms on the opposite bank—kneeling in gratitude for his deliverance from this double peril. All were struck with the piety of the youth, and earnestly rejoiced at his deliverance; though they did not presume to say so, or look as if they thought it. I never saw so changed a person as the master when he re-entered the castle gate: his cheek was blanched—his eye quelled—his fierce plume hung broken over his shoulder— his step was unequal; and in the voice of a feeble girl he said—'Bring me a cup of wine.' I was his cupbearer, and for the first time in his life he thanked me graciously, and in the warmth of his gratitude tapped my shoulder: the caress nearly hurled me across the hall. What passed in his retiring-room, I know not. Some said the 'Femme Noir' visited him again; I cannot tell, I did not see her; I speak of what I saw, not of what I heard. The storm passed away with a clap of thunder, to which the former sounds were but as the rattling pebbles beneath the swell of a summer wave. The next morning Monsieur sent for the Pasteur. The good man seemed terror-stricken as he entered the hall; but Monsieur filled him a quart of gold coins out of a leathern bag, to repair his church, and that quickly; and grasping his hand as he departed, looked him steadily in the face. As he did so, large drops stood like beads upon his brow; his stern, coarse features, were strangely moved, while he gazed upon the calm, pale minister of peace and love. 'You,' he said, 'bid God bless the poorest peasant that passes you on the mountain; have you no blessing to give the master of Rohean?'

" 'My son,' answered the good man, 'I give you the blessing I may give:—May God bless you, and may your heart be opened to give and to receive.'

" 'I know I can give,' replied the proud man; 'but what can I receive?'

" 'Love,' he replied. 'All your wealth has not brought you happiness, because you are unloving and unloved!'

"The demon returned to his brow, but it did not remain there.

" 'You shall give me lessons in this thing,' he said; and so the good man went his way.

"Amelie continued a close prisoner; but a change came over Monsieur. At first he shut himself up in his chamber, and no one was suffered to enter his presence: he took his food with his own hand from the only attendant who ventured to approach his door. He was heard walking up and down the room, day and night. When we were going to sleep, we heard his heavy tramp; at daybreak, there it was again; and those of the household who awoke at intervals during the night, said it was unceasing.

"Monsieur could read. Ah, you may smile; but in those days, and in those mountains, such men as 'the master' did not trouble themselves or others with knowledge: but the master of Rohean read both Latin and Greek, and commanded The Book he had never opened since his childhood to be brought him. It was taken out of its velvet case, and carried in forthwith; and we saw his shadow from without, like the shadow of a giant, bending over The Book; and he read in it for some days; and we greatly hoped it would soften and change his nature: and though I cannot say much for the softening, it certainly affected a great change; he no longer stalked moodily along the corridors, and banged the doors, and swore at the servants; he rather seemed possessed of a merry spirit, roaring out an old song—

'Aux bastions de Genéve, nos cannons,
Sont branquez;

> *S'il y a quelques attaque nous les feront ronfler,*
> *Viva! les cannoniers!'*

and then he would pause, and clang his hands together like a pair of cymbals, and laugh. And once, as I was passing along, he pounced out upon me, and whirled me round in a waltz, roaring at me when he let me down, to practise *that* and break my embroidery frame. He formed a band of horns and trumpets, and insisted on the goatherds and shepherds sounding *reveillés* in the mountains, and the village children beating drums;—his only idea of joy and happiness was noise. He set all the canton to work to mend the bridge, paying the workmen double wages; and he, who never entered a church before, would go to see how the labourers were getting on nearly every day. He talked and laughed a great deal to himself; and in his gaiety of heart would set the mastiffs fighting, and make excursions from home—we knowing not where he went. At last, Amelie was summoned to his presence, and he shook her and shouted, then kissed her; and hoping she would be a good girl, told her he had provided a husband for her. Amelie wept and prayed; and the master capered and sung. At last she fainted; and taking advantage of her unconsciousness, he conveyed her to the chapel; and there beside the altar stood the bridegroom—no other than Charles Le Maitre!

"They lived many happy years together; and when Monsieur was in every respect a better, though still a strange man, the 'Femme Noir' appeared again to him—once. She did so with a placid air, on a summer night, with her arm extended towards the heavens.

"The next day the muffled bell told the valley that the stormy, proud old master of Rohean had ceased to live."

The Child's Dream

Lady Wilde

The island of Innis-Sark (Shark Island) was a holy and peaceful place in old times; and so quiet that the pigeons used to come and build in a great cave by the sea, and no one disturbed them. And the holy saints of God had a monastery there, to which many people resorted from the mainland, for the prayers of the monks were powerful against sickness or evil, or the malice of an enemy.

Amongst others, there came a great and noble prince out of Munster, with his wife and children and their nurse; and they were so pleased with the island that they remained a year or more; for the prince loved fishing, and often brought his wife along with him.

One day, while they were both away, the eldest child, a beautiful boy of ten years old, begged his nurse to let him go and see the pigeon's cave, but she refused.

"Your father would be angry," she cried, "if you went without leave. Wait till he comes home, and see if he will allow you."

So when the prince returned, the boy told him how he longed to see the cave, and the father promised to bring him next day.

The morning was beautiful and the wind fair when they set off. But the child soon fell asleep in the boat, and never wakened all the time his father was fishing. The sleep, however, was troubled, and many a time he started and cried aloud. So the prince thought it better to turn the boat and land, and then the boy awoke.

After dinner the father called for the child. "Tell me, now," he said, "why was your sleep troubled, so that you cried out bitterly in your dream."

"I dreamed," said the boy, "that I stood upon a high rock, and at the bottom flowed the sea, but the waves made no noise; and as I looked down I saw fields and trees and beautiful flowers and bright birds in the branches, and I longed to go down and pluck the flowers. Then I heard a voice, saying, 'Blessed are the souls that come here, for this is heaven.'

"And in an instant I thought I was in the midst of the meadows amongst the birds and the flowers; and a lovely lady, bright as an angel, came up to me, and said, 'What brings you here, dear child; for none but the dead come here.'

"Then she left me, and I wept for her going; when suddenly all the sky grew black, and a great troup of wild wolves came round me, howling and opening their mouths wide as if to devour me. And I screamed, and tried to run, but I could not move, and the wolves came closer, and I fell down like one dead with fright, when, just then, the beautiful lady came again, and took my hand and kissed me.

" 'Fear not,' she said, 'take these flowers, they come from heaven. And I will bring you to the meadow where they grow.'

"And she lifted me up into the air, but I know nothing more; for then the boat stopped and you lifted me on shore, but my beautiful flowers must have fallen from my hands, for I never saw them more. And this is all my dream; but I would like to have my flowers again, for the lady told me they had the secret that would bring me to heaven."

The prince thought no more of the child's dream, but went off to fish next day as usual, leaving the boy in the care of his nurse. And again the child begged and prayed her so earnestly to bring him to the pigeon's cave, that at last she consented; but told him he must not go a step by himself, and she would bring two of the boys of the island to take care of him.

So they set off, the child and his little sister with the nurse. And the boy gathered wild flowers for his sister, and ran down to the edge of the cave where the cormorants were swimming; but there was no danger, for the two young islanders were minding him.

So the nurse was content, and being weary she fell asleep. And the little sister lay down beside her, and fell asleep likewise.

Then the boy called to his companions, the two young islanders, and told them he must catch the cormorants. So away they ran, down the path to the sea, hand in hand, and laughing as they went. Just then a piece of rock loosened and fell beside them, and trying to avoid it they slipped over the edge of the narrow path down a steep place, where there was nothing to hold on by except a large bush, in the middle of the way. They got hold of this, and thought they were now quite safe, but the bush was not strong enough to bear their weight, and it was torn up by the roots. And all three fell straight down into the sea and were drowned.

Now, at the sound of the great cry that came up from the waves, the nurse awoke, but saw no one. Then she woke up the little sister. "It is late," she cried, "they must have gone home. We have slept too long, it is already evening; let us hasten and overtake them, before the prince is back from the fishing."

But when they reached home the prince stood in the doorway. And he was very pale, and weeping.

"Where is my brother?" cried the little girl.

"You will never see your brother more," answered the prince. And from that day he never went fishing any more, but grew silent and thoughtful, and was never seen to smile. And in a short time he and his family quitted the island, never to return.

But the nurse remained. And some say she became a saint, for she was always seen praying and weeping by the entrance to the great sea cave. And one day, when they came to look for her, she lay dead on the rocks. And in her hand she held some beautiful strange flowers freshly gathered, with the dew on them. And no one knew how the flowers came into her dead hand. Only some fishermen told the story of how the night before they had seen a bright fairy child seated on the rocks singing; and he had a red sash tied round his waist, and a golden circlet binding his long yellow hair. And they all knew that he was the prince's son, who had been drowned in that spot just a twelvemonth before. And the people believed that he had brought the flowers from the spirit-land to the woman, and given them to her as a death sign, and a blessed token from God that her soul would be taken to heaven.

The Unquiet Dead

Lady Gregory

A good many years ago when I was but beginning my study of the folk-lore of belief, I wrote somewhere that if by an impossible miracle every trace and memory of Christianity could be swept out of the world, it would not shake or destroy at all the belief of the people of Ireland in the invisible world, the cloud of witnesses, in immortality and the life to come. For them the veil between things seen and unseen has hardly thickened since those early days of the world when the sons of God mated with the daughters of men; when angels spoke with Abraham in Hebron or with Columcille in the oakwoods of Derry, or when as an old man at my own gate told me they came and visited the Fianna, the old heroes of Ireland, "because they were so nice and so respectable". Ireland has through the centuries kept continuity of vision, the vision it is likely all nations possessed in the early days of faith. Here in Connacht there is no doubt as to the continuance of life after death. The spirit wanders for a while in that intermediate region to which mystics and theologians have given various names, and should it return and become visible those who loved it will not be afraid, but will, as I have already told, put a light in the window to guide the mother home to her child, or go out into the barley gardens in the hope of meeting a son. And if the message brought seems hardly worth the hearing, we may call to mind what Frederic Myers wrote of more instructed ghosts:

"If it was absurd to listen to Kepler because he bade the planets move in no perfect circles but in undignified ellipses, because he hastened and slackened from hour to hour what ought to be a heavenly body's ideal and unwavering speed; is it not absurder still to refuse to listen to these voices from afar, because they come stammering and wandering as in a dream confusedly instead of with a trumpet's call? Because spirits that bending to earth may undergo perhaps an earthly bewilderment and suffer unknown limitations, and half remember and half forget?"

And should they give the message more clearly who knows if it would be welcome? For the old Scotch story goes that when S. Columcille's brother Dobhran rose up from his grave and said, "Hell is not so bad as people say," the Saint cried out, "Clay, clay on Dobhran!" before he could tell any more.

❧

I was told by Mrs. Dennehy:

Those that mind the teaching of the clergy say the dead go to Limbo first and then to Purgatory and then to Hell or to Heaven. Hell is always burning and if you go there you never get out; but those that mind the old people don't believe, and I don't believe, that there is any Hell. I don't believe God Almighty would make Christians to put them into Hell afterwards.

It is what the old people say, that after death the shadow goes wandering, and the soul is weak, and the body is taking a rest. The shadow wanders for a while and it pays the debts it had to pay, and when it is free it puts out wings and flies to Heaven.

An Aran Man:

There was an old man died, and after three days he appeared in the cradle as a baby; they knew him by an old

20

look in his face, and his face being long and other things. An old woman that came into the house saw him, and she said, "He won't be with you long, he had three deaths to die, and this is the second," and sure enough he died at the end of six years.

Mrs. Martin:

There was a man beyond when I lived at Ballybron, and it was said of him that he was taken away—up before God Almighty. But the blessed Mother asked for grace for him for a year and a day. So he got it. I seen him myself, and many seen him, and at the end of the year and a day he died. And that man ought to be happy now anyway. When my own poor little girl was drowned in the well, I never could sleep but fretting, fretting, fretting. But one day when one of my little boys was taking his turn to serve the Mass he stopped on his knees without getting up. And Father Boyle asked him what did he see and he looking up. And he told him that he could see his little sister in the presence of God, and she shining like the sun. Sure enough that was a vision He had sent to comfort us. So from that day I never cried nor fretted any more.

A Herd:

Do you believe Roland Joyce was seen? Well, he was. A man I know told me he saw him the night of his death, in Esserkelly where he had a farm, and a man along with him going through the stock. And all of a sudden a train came into the field, and brought them both away like a blast of wind.

And as for old Parsons Persse of Castleboy, there's thousands of people has seen him hunting at night with his horses and his hounds and his bugle blowing. There's no mistake at all about him being there.

An Aran Woman:

There was a girl in the middle island had died, and when she was being washed, and a priest in the house, there flew by the window the whitest bird that ever was seen. And the priest said to the father: "Do not lament, unless what you like, your child's happy for ever!"

Mrs. Casey:

Near the strand there were two little girls went out to gather cow-dung. And they sat down beside a bush to rest themselves, and there they heard a groan coming from under the ground. So they ran home as fast as they could. And they were told when they went again to bring a man with them.

So the next time they went they brought a man with them, and they hadn't been sitting there long when they heard the saddest groan that ever you heard. So the man bent down and asked what was it. And a voice from below said, "Let some one shave me and get me out of this, for I was never shaved after dying." So the man went away, and the next day he brought soap and all that was needful and there he found a body lying laid out on the grass. So he shaved it, and with that wings came and carried it up to high heaven.

A Chimney-sweep:

I don't believe in all I hear, or I'd believe in ghosts and faeries, with all the old people telling you stories about them and the priests believing in them too. Surely the priests believe in ghosts, and tell you that they are souls that died in trouble. But I have been unabout the country night and day, and I remember when I used to have to put my hand out at the top of every chimney in Coole House; and I seen or felt nothing to frighten me, except one night two rats caught in a trap at Roxborough; and the old butler came down and beat me with a belt for the scream I gave at that. But if I believed in any one coming back, it would be in what you often hear, of a mother coming back to care for her child.

And there's many would tell you that every time you see a tree shaking there's a ghost in it.

Old Lambert of Dangan was a terror for telling stories; he told me long ago how he was near the Piper's gap on Ballybrit race-course, and he saw one riding to meet him, and it was old Michael Lynch of Ballybrista, that was dead long before, and he never would go on the race-course again. And he had heard the car with headless horses driving through Loughrea. From every part they are said to drive, and the place they are all going to is Benmore, near Loughrea, where there is a ruined dwelling-house and an old forth. And at Mount Mahon a herd told me the other day he often saw old Andrew Mahon riding about at night. But if I was a herd and saw that I'd hold my tongue about it.

Mrs. Casey:
At the graveyard of Drumacoo often spirits do be seen. Old George Fitzgerald is seen by many. And when they go up to the stone he's sitting on, he'll be sitting somewhere else.

There was a man walking in the wood near there, and he met a woman, a stranger, and he said, "Is there anything I can do for you?" For he thought she was some country-woman gone astray. "There is," says she. "Then come home with me," says he, "and tell me about it." "I can't do that," says she, "but what you can do is this, go tell my friends I'm in great trouble, for twenty times in my life I missed going to church, and they must say twenty Masses for me now to deliver me, but they seem to have forgotten me. And another thing is," says she, "there's some small debts I left and they're not paid, and those are helping to keep me in trouble." Well, the man went on and he didn't know what in the world to do, for he couldn't know who she was, for they are not permitted to tell their name. But going about visiting at country houses he used to tell the story, and at last it came out she was one of the Shannons. For at a house he was telling it at they remembered that an old woman they had, died a year ago, and that she used to be running up little debts unknown to them. So they made inquiry at Findlater's and at another shop that's done away with now, and they found that sure enough she had left some small debts, not more than ten shillings in each, and when she died no more had been said about it. So they paid these and said the Masses, and shortly after she appeared to the man again. "God bless you now," she said, "for what you did for me, for now I'm at peace."

A Tinker's Daughter:

I heard of what happened to a family in the town. One night a thing that looked like a goose came in. And when they said nothing to it, it went away up the stairs with a noise like lead. Surely if they had questioned it, they'd have found it to be some soul in trouble.

And there was another soul came back that was in trouble because of a ha'porth of salt it owed.

And there was a priest was in trouble and appeared after death, and they had to say Masses for him, because he had done some sort of a crime on a widow.

Mrs. Farley:

One time myself I was at Killinan, at a house of the Clancys' where the father and mother had died, but it was well known they often come to look after the children. I was walking with another girl through the fields there one evening and I looked up and saw a tall woman dressed all in black, with a mantle of some sort, a wide one, over her head, and the waves of the wind were blowing it off her, so that I could hear the noise of it. All her clothes were black, and had the appearance of being new. And I asked the other girl did she see her, and she said she did not. For two that are together can never see such things, but only one of them. So when I heard she saw nothing I ran as if for my life, and the woman seemed to be coming after me, till I crossed a running stream and she had no power to cross that. And one time my brother was stopping in the same house, and one night about twelve o'clock there came a smell in the house like as if all the dead people were there. And one of the girls whose father and mother had died got up out of her bed, and began to put her clothes on, and they had to lock the doors to stop her from going away out of the house.

There was a woman I knew of that after her death was kept for seven years in a tree in Kinadyfe, and for seven years after that she was kept under the arch of the little bridge beyond Kilchriest, with the water running under her. And whether there was frost or snow she had no shelter from it, not so much as the size of a leaf.

At the end of the second seven years she came to her husband, and he passing the bridge on the way home from Loughrea, and when he felt her near him he was afraid, and he didn't stop to question her, but hurried on.

So then she came in the evening to the house of her own little girl. But she was afraid when she saw her, and fell down in a faint. And the woman's sister's child was in the house, and when the little girl told her what she saw, she said, "You must surely question her when she comes again." So she came again that night, but the little girl was afraid again when she saw her and said nothing. But the third night when she came the sister's child, seeing her own little girl was afraid, said, "God bless you, God bless you." And with that the woman spoke and said, "God bless you for saying that." And then she told her all that had happened her and where she had been all the fourteen years. And she took out of her dress a black silk handkerchief and said: "I took that from my husband's neck the day I met him on the road from Loughrea, and this very night I would have killed him, because he hurried away and would not stop to help me, but now that you have helped me I'll not harm him. But bring with you to Kilmacduagh, to the graveyard, three cross sticks with wool on them, and three glasses full of salt, and have three Masses said for me; and I'll appear to you when I am at rest." And so she did; and it was for no great thing she had done that trouble had been put upon her.

John Cloran:

That house with no roof was made a hospital of in the famine, and many died there. And one night my father was passing by and he saw some one standing all in white, and two men beside him, and he thought he knew one of the men and spoke to him and said, "Is that you, Martin?" but he never spoke nor moved. And as to the thing in white, he could not say was it man or woman, but my father never went by that place again at night.

The last person buried in a graveyard has the care of all the other souls until another is to be buried, and then the soul can go and shift for itself. It may be a week or a month or a year, but watch the place it must till another soul comes.

There was a man used to be giving short measure, not giving the full yard, and one time after his death there was a man passing the river and the horse he had would not go into it.

And he heard the voice of the tailor saying from the river he had a message to send to his wife, and to tell her not to be giving short measure, or she would be sent to the same place as himself. There was a hymn made about that.

There was a woman lived in Rathkane, alone in the house, and she told me that one night something came and lay over the bed and gave three great moans. That was all ever she heard in the house.

The shadows of the dead gather round at Samhain time to see is there any one among their friends saying a few Masses for them.

An Islander:

Down there near the point, on the 6th of March, 1883, there was a curragh upset and five boys were drowned. And a man from County Clare told me that he was on the coast that day, and that he saw them walking towards him on the Atlantic.

There is a house down there near the sea, and one day the woman of it was sitting by the fire, and a little girl came in at the door, and a red cloak about her, and she sat down by the fire. And the woman asked her where did she come from, and she said that she had just come from Connemara. And then she went out, and when she was going out the door she made herself known to her sister that was standing in it, and she called out to the mother. And when the mother knew it was the child she had lost near a year before, she ran out to call her, for she wouldn't for all the world to have not known her when she was there. But she was gone and she never came again.

There was this boy's father took a second wife, and he was walking home one evening, and his wife behind him, and there was a great wind blowing, and he kept his head stooped down because of the seaweed coming blowing into his eyes. And she was about twenty paces behind, and she saw his first wife come and walk close beside him, and he never saw her, having his head down, but she kept with him near all the way. And when they got home, she told the husband who was with him, and with the fright she got she was bad in her bed for two or three days—do you remember that, Martin? She died after, and he has a third wife taken now.

I believe all that die are brought among them, except maybe an odd old person.

A Kildare Woman:

There was a woman I knew sent into the Rotunda Hospital for an operation. And when she was going she cried when she was saying good-bye to her cousin that was a friend of mine, for she felt in her that she would not come back again. And she put her two arms about her going away and said, "If the dead can do any good thing for the living, I'll do it for you." And she never recovered, but died in the hospital. And within a few weeks something came on her cousin, my friend, and they said it was her side that was paralysed, and she died. And many said it was no common illness, but that it was the dead woman that had kept to her word.

A Connemara Man:

There was a boy in New York was killed by rowdies, they killed him standing against a lamppost and he was frozen to it, and stood there till morning. And it is often since that time he was seen in the room and the passages of the house where he used to be living.

And in the house beyond a woman died, and some other family came to live in it; but every night she came back and stripped the clothes off them, so at last they went away.

When some one goes that owes money, the weight of the soul is more than the weight of the body, and it can't get away and keeps wandering till some one has courage to question it.

Mrs. Casey:

My grandmother told my mother that in her time at Cloughballymore, there was a woman used to appear in the churchyard of Rathkeale, and that many boys and girls and children died with the fright they got when they saw her.

So there was a gentleman living near was very sorry for all the children dying, and he went to an old woman to ask her was there any way to do away with the spirit that appeared. So she said if any one would have courage to go and to question it, he could do away with it. So the gentleman went at midnight and waited at the churchyard, and he on his horse, and had a sword with him. So presently the shape appeared and he called to it and said, "Tell me what you are?" And it came over to him, and when he saw the face he got such a fright that he turned the horse's head and galloped away as hard as he could. But after galloping a long time he looked down and what did he see beside him but the woman running and her hand on the horse. So he took his sword and gave a slash at her, and cut through her arm, so that she gave a groan and vanished, and he went on home.

And when he got to the stable and had the lantern lighted, you may think what a start he got when he saw the hand still holding on to the horse, and no power could lift it off. So he went into the house and said his prayers to Almighty God to take it off. And all night long, he could hear moaning and crying about the house. And in the morning when he went out the hand was gone, but all the stable was splashed with blood. But the woman was never seen in those parts again.

A Seaside Man:

And many see the faeries at Knock and there was a carpenter died, and he could be heard all night in his shed making coffins and carts and all sorts of things, and the people are afraid to go near it. There were four boys from Knock drowned five years ago, and often now they are seen walking on the strand and in the fields and about the village.

There was a man used to go out fowling, and one day his sister said to him, "Whatever you do don't go out tonight and don't shoot any wild-duck or any birds you see flying— for tonight they are all poor souls travelling."

An Old Man in Galway Workhouse:

Burke of Carpark's son died, but he used often to be seen going about afterwards. And one time a herd of his father's met with him and he said, "Come tonight and help us against the hurlers from the north, for they have us beat twice, and if they beat us a third time, it will be a bad year for Ireland."

It was in the daytime they had the hurling match through the streets of Galway. No one could see them, and no one could go outside the door while it lasted, for there went such a whirlwind through the town that you could not look through the window.

And he sent a message to his father that he would find some paper he was looking for a few days before, behind a certain desk, between it and the wall, and the father found it there. He would not have believed it was his son the herd met only for that.

A Munster Woman:
I have only seen them myself like dark shadows, but there's many can see them as they are. Surely they bring away the dead among them.

There was a woman in County Limerick that died after her baby being born. And all the people were in the house when the funeral was to be, crying for her. And the cars and the horses were out on the road. And there was seen among them a carriage full of ladies, and with them the woman was sitting that they were crying for, and the baby with her, and it dressed.

And there was another woman I knew of died, and left a family, and often after, the people saw her in their dreams, and always in rich clothes, though all the clothes she had were given away after she died, for the good of her soul, except maybe her shawl. And her husband married a serving girl after that, and she was hard to the children, and one night the woman came back to her, and had like to throw her out of the window in her nightdress, till she gave a promise to treat the children well, and she was afraid not to treat them well after that.

There was a farmer died and he had done some man out of a saddle, and he came back after to a friend, and gave him no rest till he gave a new saddle to the man he had cheated.

Mrs. Casey:
There was a woman my brother told me about and she had a daughter that was red-haired. And the girl got married

when she was under twenty, for the mother had no man to tend the land, so she thought best to let her go. And after her baby being born, she never got strong but stopped in the bed, and a great many doctors saw her but did her no good.

And one day the mother was at Mass at the chapel and she got a start, for she thought she saw her daughter come in to the chapel with the same shawl and clothes on her that she had before she took to the bed, but when they came out from the chapel, she wasn't there. So she went to the house, and asked was she after going out, and what they told her was as if she got a blow, for they said the girl hadn't ten minutes to live, and she was dead before ten minutes were out. And she appears now sometimes; they see her drawing water from the well at night and bringing it into the house, but they find nothing there in the morning.

A Connemara Man:

There was a man had come back from Boston, and one day he was out in the bay, going towards Aran with £3 worth of cable he was after getting from McDonagh's store in Galway. And he was steering the boat, and there were two turf-boats along with him, and all in a minute they saw he was gone, swept off the boat with a wave and it a dead calm.

And they saw him come up once, straight up as if he was pushed, and then he was brought down again and rose no more.

And it was some time after that a friend of his in Boston, and that was coming home to this place, was in a crowd of people out there. And he saw him coming to him and he said, "I heard that you were drowned," and the man said, "I am not dead, but I was brought here, and when you go home, bring these three guineas to McDonagh in Galway for it's owed him for the cable I got from him." And he put the three guineas in his hand and vanished away.

An Old Army Man:

I have seen Hell myself. I had a sight of it one time in a vision. It had a very high wall around it, all of metal, and an archway in the wall, and a straight walk into it, just like what would be leading into a gentleman's orchard, but the edges were not trimmed with box but with red-hot metal. And inside the wall there were cross walks, and I'm not sure what there was to the right, but to the left there was five great furnaces and they full of souls kept there with great chains. So I turned short and went away; and in turning I looked again at the wall and I could see no end to it.

And another time I saw Purgatory. It seemed to be in a level place and no walls around it, but it all one bright blaze, and the souls standing in it. And they suffer near as much as in Hell, only there are no devils with them there, and they have the hope of Heaven.

And I heard a call to me from there "Help me to come out of this!" And when I looked it was a man I used to know in the army, an Irishman and from this country, and I believe him to be a descendant of King O'Connor of Athenry. So I stretched out my hand first but then I called out, "I'd be burned in the flames before I could get within three yards of you." So then he said, "Well, help me with your prayers," and so I do.

The Woman with the Hood

L. T. Meade

It was late in the October of a certain year when I was asked to become "*locum tenens*" to a country practitioner in one of the midland counties. He was taken ill and obliged to leave home hastily. I therefore entered on my duties without having any indication of the sort of patients whom I was to visit. I was a young man at the time, and a great enthusiast with regard to the medical profession. I believed in personal influence and the magnetism of a strong personality as being all-conducive to the furtherance of the curative art. I had no experience, however, to guide me with regard to country patients, my work hitherto having been amongst the large population of a manufacturing town. On the very night of my arrival my first experience as a country doctor began. I had just got into bed, and was dozing off into a sound sleep, when the night bell which hung in my room rang pretty sharply. I jumped up and went to the tube, calling down to ask what was the matter.

"Are you the new doctor?" asked the voice.

"Yes, my name is Bruce; who wants me?"

"Mrs. Frayling of Garth Hall. The young lady is very bad. I have got a trap here; how soon can you be ready?"

"In a couple of minutes," I answered. I hastily got into my clothes, and in less than five minutes had mounted beside a rough-looking man, into a high gig. He touched his horse, who bounded off, at a great speed, and I found myself rattling through the country in the dead of night.

"How far off is the Hall?" I asked.

"A matter of two miles," was the reply.

"Do you know anything of the nature of the young lady's illness?"

"Yes I do; it is the old thing."

"Can you not enlighten me?" I asked, seeing that the man had shut up his lips and employed himself flicking his horse with the end of his long whip. The beast flew faster and faster, the man turned and fixed his eyes full upon me in the moonlight.

"They'll tell you when you get there," he said. "All I can say is that you will do no good, no one can, the matter ain't in our province. We are turning into the avenue now; you will soon know for yourself."

We dashed down a long avenue, and drew up in a couple of moments at a door sheltered by a big porch. I saw a tall lady in evening dress standing in the brightly lighted hall within.

"Have you brought the doctor, Thompson?" I heard her say to the man who had driven me.

"Yes, ma'am," was the reply. "The new doctor, Doctor Bruce."

"Oh! Then Dr. Mackenzie has really left?"

"He left this morning, ma'am, I told you so."

I heard her utter a slight sigh of disappointment.

"Come this way, Dr. Bruce," she said. "I am sorry to have troubled you."

She led me as she spoke across the hall and into a drawing-room of lofty dimensions, beautifully furnished in modern style. It was now between one and two in the morning, but the whole house was lit up as if the night were several hours younger. Mrs. Frayling wore a black evening dress, low to the neck and with demi sleeves. She had dark eyes and a beautiful, kindly face. It looked haggard now and alarmed.

"The fact is," she said, "I have sent for you on a most extraordinary mission. I do not know that I should have troubled a strange doctor, but I hoped that Dr. Mackenzie had not yet left."

"He left this morning," I said. "He was very ill; a case of nervous breakdown. He could not even wait to give me instructions with regard to my patients."

"Ah, yes," she said averting her eyes from mine as she spoke. "Our doctor used to be as hale a man as could be found in the country round. Nervous breakdown; I think I understand. I hope, Dr. Bruce, that you are not troubled by nerves."

"Certainly not," I answered. "As far as I am concerned they don't exist. Now what can I do for you, Mrs. Frayling?"

"I want you to see my daughter. I want you to try and quiet her terrors. Dr. Mackenzie used to be able to do so, but of late—"

"Her terrors!" I said. "I must ask you to explain further."

"I am going to do so. My daughter, Lucy, she is my only child, is sorely troubled by the appearance of an apparition."

I could scarcely forbear from smiling.

"Your daughter wants change," I said, "change of scene and air."

"That is the queer thing," said Mrs. Frayling; "she will not take change, nothing will induce her to leave Garth Hall; and yet living here is slowly but surely bringing her either to her grave or to a worse fate, that of a lunatic asylum. She went to bed to-night as usual, but an hour afterwards I was awakened by her screams; I ran to her room and found her sitting up in bed, trembling violently. Her eyes were fixed on a certain part of the room; they were wide open, and had a look of the most horrified agony in them which

I have never seen in the human face. She did not see me when I went into the room, but when I touched her hand she clasped it tightly.

" 'Tell her to go away, mother,' she said, 'she won't stir for me; I cannot speak to her, I have not the courage, and she is waiting for me to speak; tell her to go away, mother—tell her to cease to trouble me—tell her to go.'

"I could see nothing, Dr. Bruce, but she continued to stare just towards the foot of her bed, and described the terrible thing which was troubling her.

" 'Can't you see her yourself?' she said. 'She is a dead woman, and she comes here night after night—see her yellow face—oh, mother, tell her to go—tell her to go!'

"I did what I could for my poor child, but no words of mine could soothe or reassure her. The room was bright with firelight, and there were several candles burning, I could not see a soul. At last the poor girl fainted off with terror. I then sent a messenger for Dr. Mackenzie. She now lies moaning in her bed, our old nurse is sitting with her. She is terribly weak, and drops of agony are standing on her forehead. She cannot long continue this awful strain."

"It must be a case of delusion," I said. "You say you saw nothing in the room?"

"Nothing; but it is only right to tell you that the house is haunted."

I smiled, and fidgeted in my chair.

"Ah! I know," said Mrs. Frayling, "that you naturally do not believe in ghosts and apparitions, but perhaps you would change your mind if you lived long at Garth Hall. I have lived here for the last twelve years, and can certainly testify to the fact of having heard most unaccountable sounds, but I have never seen anything. My daughter, Lucy, has been educated abroad, and did not come to Garth Hall to live until three months ago; it was soon after this that the apparition began to appear to her. Now it is her nightly torment, and it is simply killing her, and yet she refuses to go. Every day she says to me, 'I know, mother, that that awful spirit is in fearful trouble, and perhaps to-night I may have the courage to speak to it,' but night after night much the same thing takes place; the poor child endures the agony until she faints right off, and each day her nerves are weaker and her whole strength more completely shattered."

"Well, I will go up now and see the patient," I said. "It is of course nothing whatever but a case of strong delusion, and against her will, Mrs. Frayling, it is your duty to remove your daughter from this house immediately."

"You will tell a different story after you have seen her," said the mother.

She rose as she spoke and conducted me up some shallow bright-looking stairs. She then led me into a large bedroom on the first landing. The fire burned brightly in the grate, and four or five candles stood about in different directions. Their light fell full upon the form of a very young and extremely beautiful girl.

Her face was as white as the pillow on which it rested; her eyes were shut, and the dark fringe of her long eyelashes rested on her cheeks; her hair was tossed over the pillow; her hands, thin to emaciation, lay outside the coverlet; now and then her fingers worked convulsively.

Bending gently forward I took her wrist between my finger and thumb. The pulse was very faint and slow. As I was feeling it she opened her eyes.

"Who are you?" she asked, looking at me without any alarm, and with only a very languid curiosity in her tone.

"I am the new doctor who has come in Dr. Mackenzie's place," I answered. "My name is Bruce."

She gave me just the ghost of a smile.

"Mine is not a case for the doctor," she said. "Has mother told you what troubles me?"

"Yes," I answered. "You are very nervous and must not be alone. I will sit with you for a little."

"It makes no difference whether you are here or not," she said. "She will come back again in about an hour. You may or may not see her. She will certainly come, and then my awful terrors will begin again."

"Well, we will wait for her together," I said, as cheerfully as I could.

I moved a chair forward as I spoke and sat down by the bedside.

Miss Frayling shut her eyes with a little impatient gesture. I motioned to Mrs. Frayling to seat herself not far away; and going deliberately to some of the candles put them out. The light no longer fell strongly on the bed—the patient was in shadow. I hoped she might fall into really deep slumber and not awaken till the morning light had banished ghostly terrors. She certainly seemed to have sunk into gentle and calm sleep; the expression of her face seemed to smooth out, her brow was no longer corrugated with anxious wrinkles—gentle smiles played about her lips. She looked like the child she was. I guessed as I watched her that her years could not number more than seventeen or eighteen.

"She is better," said Mrs. Frayling. "She may not have another attack to-night." As she spoke she rose, and telling me she would return in a few minutes, left the room. She and I were the only watchers by the sick girl, the servants having retired to bed. Mrs. Frayling went to fetch something. She had scarcely done so before I was conscious of a complete change in the aspect of the room—it had felt home-like, warm, and comfortable up to this moment; now I was distinctly conscious of a sense of chill. I could not account for my sensations, but most undoubtedly my heart began to beat more quickly than was quite agreeable; I felt a creeping sensation down my back—the cold seemed to grow greater.

I said to myself, "The fire wants replenishing," but I had an unaccountable aversion to stirring; I did not even want to turn my head. At the same moment Miss Frayling, who had been sleeping so peacefully, began evidently to dream; her face worked with agitation; she suddenly opened her eyes and uttered a sharp, piercing cry.

"Keep her back," she said, flinging out her arms, as if she wanted to push something from her.

I started up instantly, and went to the bedside.

At this moment Mrs. Frayling came into the room. The moment she did so the sense of chill and unaccountable horror left me; the room became once more warm and home-like. I looked at the fire, it was piled up high in the grate and was burning merrily. Miss Frayling, however, did not share my pleasanter sensations.

"I said she would come back," she exclaimed, pointing with her finger to the foot of the bed.

I looked in that direction but could see nothing.

"Can't you see her? Oh, I wish you could see her," she cried. "She stands there at the foot of the bed; she wears a hood, and her face is yellow. She has been dead a long time, and I know she wants to say something. I cannot speak to her. Oh, tell her to go away; tell her to go away."

"Shut your eyes, Miss Frayling; do not look," I said.

Then I turned and boldly faced the empty space where the excited girl had seen the apparition.

"Whoever you are, leave us now," I said in an authoritative voice. "We are not prepared for you to-night. Leave us now."

To my surprise Miss Frayling gave a gleeful laugh.

"Why, she has gone," she exclaimed in a voice of relief. "She walked out of the door—I saw her go. I don't believe she will come back at present. How queer! Then you did see her, Dr. Bruce?"

"No,' I answered; "I saw nothing."

"But she heard you; she nodded her head once and then went. She will come back again, of course; but perhaps not to-night. I don't feel frightened any longer. I believe I shall sleep."

She snuggled down under the bedclothes.

"Have some of this beef-tea, Lucy," said her mother, bringing a cup to the bedside. It was steaming hot, she had gone away to warm it.

"Yes, I feel faint and hungry," replied the girl; she raised her pretty head and allowed her mother to feed and pet her.

"I am much better," she said. "I know she won't come back again to-night; you need not stay with me any longer, Dr. Bruce."

"I will stay with her, Doctor; you must lie down in another room," said the mother.

I consented to go as far as the ante-room. There was a comfortable sofa there, and I had scarcely laid my head upon it before I fell into a sound slumber.

When I awakened it was broad daylight and Mrs. Frayling was standing over me.

"Lucy is much better and is getting up," she said. "She looks almost herself. What an extraordinary effect your words had, Dr. Bruce."

"They came as a sort of inspiration," I said; "I did not mean them to be anything special."

"Then you do not believe that she really saw the apparition?"

"Certainly not; her brain is very much excited and overwrought. You ought to take her away to-day."

"That is the queer thing," said Mrs. Frayling. "I told you that she would not consent to leave the house, believing, poor child, that her mission was to try and comfort this awful ghost, in case she could summon courage to speak to it. She told me this morning, however, that she was quite willing to go and suggested that we should sleep at the Metropole in town to-night."

"The best thing possible," I said. "Take her away immediately. Give her plenty of occupation and variety, and let her see heaps of cheerful people. She will doubtless soon get over her terrors."

"It is very strange," repeated Mrs. Frayling. "Her attitude of mind seems completely altered. She wishes to see you for a moment before you leave us. I will meet you in the breakfast-room in a quarter of an hour, Dr. Bruce."

I made a hasty toilet and followed Mrs. Frayling downstairs. We ate breakfast almost in silence, and just before the meal was over Miss Frayling made her appearance. She was a very slightly-built girl, tall and graceful as a reed. She came straight up to me.

"I don't know how to thank you," she said, holding out her hand.

"Why?" I asked in astonishment. "I am glad I was able to relieve you, but I am rather puzzled to know what great thing I really did."

"Why, don't you know?" she answered. "Can't you guess? She will come to you now. I don't believe she will trouble me any more."

"Well, I am stronger to receive her than you are," I said, smiling and trying to humour the girl's fancy.

Soon afterwards I took my leave and returned to Dr. Mackenzie's house. I spent the day without anything special occurring, and in the evening, being dead tired, went to bed as usual. Dr. Mackenzie's house was an essentially modern one. Anything less ghostly than the squarely-built cheerful rooms could scarcely be imagined. I was alone in the house with the exception of his servants. I went to bed, and had scarcely laid my head on the pillow before I was sound asleep. I was suddenly awakened out of my first slumbers by someone calling to me through the speaking-tube.

"Yes, I will come immediately," I answered.

I sprang out of bed and applied my ear to the tube. "You are wanted at Garth Hall," said the voice.

"But surely there is no one ill there to-night?" I said.

"You are wanted immediately; come without delay," was the reply.

"I will be with you in a minute," I answered.

I felt almost annoyed, but there was no help for it. I hurried into my clothes and went downstairs.

"How very silly of Mrs. Frayling not to have taken her daughter away—shall I have to go through a repetition of last night's scene over again?" I thought.

I opened the hall door, expecting to see a horse and gig, and the man who had driven me the night before. To my astonishment there was not a soul in sight.

"What can this mean?" I said to myself. "Has the messenger been careless enough not to bring a trap—it will be very troublesome if I have to get my own horse out at this hour—where can the man be?"

I looked to right and left—the night was a moonlit one—there was not a soul in sight. Very much provoked, but never for a moment doubting that I was really summoned, I went off to the stables, saddled Dr. Mackenzie's horse, Rover, and mounting, rode off to Garth Hall. The hour was quite late, between twelve and one o'clock. When I drew up at the door the house was in total darkness.

"What can this mean?" I said to myself. I rang a bell fiercely, and after a long time a servant put her head out of an upper window.

"Who is there?" she asked.

"I—Dr. Bruce," I cried. "I have been sent for in a hurry to see Miss Frayling."

"Good Lord!" I heard the woman exclaim. "Wait a minute, sir, and I will come down to you," she shouted.

In a couple of minutes the great hall door was unchained and unlocked, and a respectable middle-aged woman stood on the steps.

"Miss Frayling has gone to London with her mother, sir," she said. "You are quite certain you were sent for?"

"Quite," I answered. "Your man—the man who came last night—"

"Not Thompson!" she cried.

"Yes, the same man called for me through the speaking-tube to come here at once—he said Miss Frayling was ill, and wanted me."

"It must have been a hoax, sir," said the housekeeper, but I noticed a troubled and perplexed look on her face. "I am very sorry indeed, but Miss Frayling is not here—we do not expect the ladies back for some weeks," she added.

"I am sorry I troubled you," I answered; I turned my horse's head and went home again.

The next day I set enquiries on foot with regard to the hoax which had been played upon me. Whoever had done the trick, no one was ready to own to it, and I noticed that the servants looked mysterious and nodded their heads when I said it was to Garth Hall I had been summoned.

The next night the same thing occurred. My night bell was rung and a voice shouted to me through the speaking-tube to come immediately to Garth Hall. I took no notice whatever of the trick, but determined to lay a trap for the impertinent intruder on my repose for the following night. I had a very savage dog, and I tied him outside the house. My housekeeper also agreed to sit up. Between twelve and one o'clock I was called again. I flew to my window and looked out. There was not a soul in sight, but a queer sense of indescribable chill and unaccountable horror took sudden possession of me. The dog was crouching down on the ground with his face hidden in his paws; he was moaning feebly. I dressed, went downstairs, unchained him and brought him up to my room. He crept on to my bed and lay there trembling; I will own to the fact that his master shared the unaccountable horror. What was the matter? I dared not answer this question even to myself. Mrs. Marks, my housekeeper, looked very solemn and grave the next morning.

"Sir," she said, when she brought in breakfast, "if I were you, I would go away from here. There is something very queer at the Hall and it seems to me—but there, I cannot speak of it."

"There are some things best not spoken of," I said shortly; "whoever is playing me a hoax has not chosen to reveal himself or herself. We can best tire the unlucky individual out by taking no notice."

"Yes, sir, perhaps that is best. Now I have got some news for you."

"What is that?" I asked.

"Mrs. and Miss Frayling returned to the Hall this morning."

"This morning!" I exclaimed, in astonishment, "but it is not yet nine o'clock."

"True, sir, but early as the hour is they passed this house not half-an-hour ago in the closed brougham. Miss Frayling looked very white, and the good lady, her mother, full of anxiety. I caught a glimpse of them as I was cleaning the steps; I doubt not, sir, but you will be summoned to the Hall to-day."

"Perhaps so," I answered briefly.

Mrs. Marks looked at me as if she would say something further, but refrained, and to my relief soon afterwards left me alone.

I finished my breakfast and went out about my daily rounds. I do not think myself destitute of pluck but I cannot pretend that I liked the present position. What was the mystery? What horrible dark joke was being played? With my healthy bringing up I could not really ascribe the thing to supernatural agency. A trick there was, of course. I vowed that I would find it out before I was much older, but then I remembered the chill and the terror which had assailed me when sitting up with Miss Frayling. The same chill and terror had come over me when I suddenly opened my window the night before.

"The best thing I can do is not to think of this," I commented, and then I absorbed myself with my patients.

Nothing occurred of any moment that day, nor was I summoned to attend the ladies at Garth Hall. About ten o'clock that night I had to go out to attend a farmer's wife who was suddenly taken ill. I sat with her for a little time and did not return till about half-past eleven. I then went straight up to my room and went to bed. I had scarcely fallen into my first slumber when I was aroused by the sharp ringing of my night bell. I felt inclined for a moment not to pay the least attention to it, but as it rang again with a quick imperative sound, I got up, more from the force of habit than anything else, and calling through the speaking-tube, applied my ear to it.

"Dr. Bruce, will you come at once to Garth Hall?" called a voice.

"No, I will not," I called back in reply.

There was a pause below, evidently of astonishment—and then the voice called again.

"I don't think you quite understand, sir. Mrs. Frayling wants you to visit Miss Frayling immediately; the young lady is very ill."

I was about to put the cap on the tube and return to my bed when I distinctly heard the crunch of wheels beneath my window and the pawing of an impatient horse. I crossed the room, threw open the window and looked out. A horse and gig were now standing under the window, and the man, Thompson, who had summoned me on the first night, was staring up at me.

"For God's sake, come, sir," he said. "The young lady is mortal bad."

"I will be with you in a minute," I said. I dressed myself trembling.

In an incredibly short space of time Thompson and I arrived at the Hall. Through our entire drive the man never spoke, but when we drew up at the great porch he uttered a heavy sigh of relief and muttered the words: "The devil is in this business. I don't pretend to understand it."

I looked at him, but resolved to take no notice of his queer remark. Mrs. Frayling met me on the steps.

"Come in at once," she said. She took both my hands in hers and drew me into the house. We entered her cheerful drawing-room. The poor lady's face was ghastly, her eyes full not only of trouble, but of horror.

"Now, Dr. Bruce," she said, "you must do your best."

"In what way?" I said.

"I fear my poor girl is mad. Unless you can manage to relieve her mind, she certainly will be by morning."

"Tell me what has happened since I last saw you, as briefly as possible," I said.

"I will do so," she replied. "Acting on your instructions, Lucy and I went to the Metropole. She was quite happy on the first day, but in the middle of the night grew very much disturbed. She and I were sleeping together. She awakened me and told me that the apparition at Garth Hall was pulling her—that the woman in the hood was imperatively demanding her presence.

" 'I know what has happened.' said Lucy. 'Dr. Bruce has refused to help her. She has gone to him but he won't respond to her efforts to bring him on the scene. How cruel he is!'

"I soothed the poor child as best I could, and towards morning she dropped off asleep. The next night she was in a still greater state of terror, again assuring me that the lady in the hood was drawing her, and that you, Dr. Bruce, were turning a deaf ear to her entreaties. On the third night she became almost frantic.

" 'I must go back,' she said. 'My spirit is being torn out of my body. If I am not back at Garth Hall early in the morning I shall die.'

"Her distress and horror were so extreme that I had to humour her. We took the very earliest train from London, and arrived at the Hall at nine o'clock. During the day Lucy was gentle and subdued; she seemed relieved at being back again, told me that she would go early to bed and that she hoped that she might have a good night. About an hour ago I heard her screaming violently, and, rushing to her room, found her in almost a state of collapse from horror—she kept pointing in a certain direction, but could not speak. I sent Thompson off in a hurry for you. As soon as ever I said I would do so she became a little better, and said she would dress herself. It is her intention now to ask you to spend the night with us, and, if possible, speak again to the horrible thing which is driving my child into a madhouse."

"I will tell you something strange," I said, when Mrs. Frayling paused, "I was undoubtedly called during the last three nights. A voice shouted through my speaking-tube, desiring me to come to Garth Hall. On the first night I went, feeling sure that I was really summoned; since then I have believed that it was a hoax."

"Oh, this is awful," said Mrs. Frayling, trembling excessively; she turned and asked me to follow her upstairs. We entered the same spacious and cheerful bedroom;

Lucy Frayling was now pacing up and down in front of the fireplace; she did not notice either of us when we came in; the expression on her face was almost that of an insane person. The pupils of her eyes were widely dilated.

"Lucy," said her mother, "Here is Dr. Bruce."

She paused when my name was mentioned and looked at me fixedly. Her eyes grew dark with anger—she clenched her hand.

"You were faithless," she said; "she wanted you, and you would not accept the burden; you told me when last I saw you that you were glad she turned to you, for you are stronger than me, but you are a coward."

"Come, come," I said, trying to speak cheerfully. "I am here now, and will do anything you wish."

"I will prove you," said Miss Frayling, in an eager voice. "She will come again presently; when she comes, will you speak to her?"

"Certainly," I replied, "but remember I may not see her."

"I will tell you when she appears; I will point with my hand—I may not have power to utter words—but I will point to where she stands. When I do, speak to her; ask her why she troubles us—promise—you spoke once, speak again."

"I promise," I replied, and my voice sounded solemn and intense.

Miss Frayling heaved a deep sigh of relief, she went and stood by the mantelpiece with her back to the fire. I sat down on the nearest chair, and Mrs. Frayling followed my example. The clock ticked loudly on the mantelpiece, the candles burned with a steady gleam, the fire threw out cheerful flames, all was silent in the chamber. There was not a stir, not a sound. The minutes flew on. Miss Frayling stood as quiet as if she were turned into stone; suddenly she spoke,

"There is an adverse influence here," she said. "Mother, will you go into the ante-room. You can leave the door open, but will you stay in the ante-room for a little?"

Mrs. Frayling glanced at me; I nodded to her to comply. She left the room, going into a pretty little boudoir out of which the bedroom opened. I could see her from where I sat. Lucy now slightly altered her position. I saw that her eyes were fixed in the direction of another door, which opened from the outside corridor into the room. I tried to speak, to say something cheerful, but she held up her finger to stop me.

"She is coming," she said, in a stifled voice. "I feel the first stirring of the indescribable agony which always heralds her approach. Oh, my God, help me to endure. Was ever girl tortured as I am, before?"

She wrung her slight hands, her brows were knit, I saw the perspiration standing in great drops on her brow. I thought she would faint, and was about to rise to administer some restorative, when in the far distance I distinctly heard a sound; it was the sound of a woman's footsteps. It came along, softly tapping on the floor as it came; I heard the swish of a dress, the sound came nearer, the handle of the door was turned, I started and looked round. I did not see anybody, but immediately the room was filled with that sense of cold and chill which I had twice before experienced. My heart beat to suffocation, I felt my tongue cleave to the roof of my mouth. I was so overpowered by my own sensations that I had no time to watch Miss Frayling. Suddenly I heard her utter a low groan. I made a violent effort and turned my face in her direction. The poor girl was staring straight before her as if she were turned into stone. Her eyes were fixed in the direction of the door.

She raised her hand slowly and tremblingly, and pointed in the direction where her eyes were fixed. I looked across the room. Was it fancy, or was I conscious of a faint blue mist where no mist ought to be? I am not certain on that point, but I know at the same moment the horror which had almost overbalanced my reason suddenly left me. I found my voice.

"What do you want?" I said. "Why do you trouble us? What is the matter?"

The words had scarcely passed my lips before Miss Frayling's face underwent a queer change; she was also relieved from the agony of terror which was overmastering her.

"She is beckoning," she said; "come quickly."

She sprang across the room as she spoke, and seized a candle.

"Come at once," she said in a breathless voice, "she is beckoning—come."

Miss Frayling ran out of the room; I followed her, and Mrs. Frayling, who had come to the door while this strange scene was going on, accompanied us. Miss Frayling still taking the lead, we went downstairs. The whole house was full of strange unaccountable chill. We entered the upper hall, and then turning to our left, went down some steep stairs which led into a cellar.

"Where are you going now?" asked Mrs. Frayling.

"Come on, mother, come on," called Lucy, she will tell us what to do."

We turned at the foot of the stairs into a low arched room with one tiny window. There was a heavy buttress of wall here which bulged out in unaccountable manner. The moment we entered this room, Lucy turned and faced us.

"She has gone in there," she said—"right into the wall."

"Well," I said, "now that we have followed her, let us go back—it is cold in the cellar."

Miss Frayling laughed hysterically.

"Do you think," she said, "that I will go back now? We must have this opened—can you do it, Dr. Bruce? Can you do it now, this moment? Mother, are there tools anywhere?"

"Not now, dear, not to-night," said the mother.

"Yes, to-night, this moment," exclaimed the girl. "Let Thompson be called—we have not a moment to lose. She went in right through this wall and smiled at me as she went. Poor, poor ghost! I believe her sad wanderings are nearly over."

"What are we to do?" said Mrs. Frayling, turning to me.

"We will open the wall at once," I said. "It will not be difficult to remove a few bricks. If you will kindly tell me where Thompson is I will fetch him."

"No, I will go for him myself," said Mrs. Frayling.

She left the cellar, returning in the space of a few minutes with the man. He brought a crowbar and other tools with him. He and I quickly removed some bricks. As soon as we had done so we found an empty space inside, into which we could thrust our hands. We made it a little larger and then were able to insert a candle. Lying on the floor within this space was a human skeleton.

I cried out at the awful discovery we had made, but Miss Frayling showed neither surprise nor terror.

"Poor ghost!" repeated the girl; "she will rest now. It was worth all this fearful suffering to bring her rest at last."

The discovery of the skeleton was the topic of the neighbourhood. It was given a Christian burial in due course, and from that hour to this the ghost at Garth Hall has never appeared.

I cannot pretend to account for this story in any way—no one has ever found out why those human bones were built into the old wall. The whole thing is queer and uncomfortable, a phenomenon which will not be explained on this side of Eternity.

The Wee Gray Woman

Ethna Carbery

His cabin stood by the side of a burn into which the sally-trees drooped from either side, making a thick fringe of green that met overhead and cast dappled shadows on the clear water when the sun stood high and fierce in the heavens. Little ripples broke in white bubbles around the stones that made the crossing-places, and the speckled trout darted like tiny silver spears through their haunts below the overhanging banks.

It was a tranquil, lonely spot; eerie, too, in the autumn twilight, when the slow-creeping mists rose up from the bog for miles around, and many were the tales told of an evening, by the folk living on the high land, of lights that flashed all over the bog at the very moment that Jamie Boyson set his candle in his cottage window to guide the Wee Gray Woman up the rugged loaning to her seat in the chimney corner.

Once it happened that the wild young fellows of Glenwherry came in the dead of night to play a trick on Jamie. They stole over the stepping-stones of the burn and noiselessly reached the one-paned window, half hidden by thatch, in which the light gleamed. A red turf fire blazing on the hearth lit up the interior of the old man's kitchen; it shone on the battered ancient dresser, and on the store of carefully-kept delf that had been his mother's. For Jamie had the name of being cleanly and thrifty in his ways. The hearth was carefully swept, the flat stones at front and sides whitened by a practised hand, and no ragged streaks wandered over the edges on to the clay floor beyond. A three-legged stool stood in front of the fire, placed there for the convenience of the unearthly visitant who, Jamie said, came nightly to sit and rest herself by the *greesaugh* until the black cock should crow in the rafters above the settle-bed, invariably awaking him at the same moment that the Wee Gray Woman got warning to leave. That was why he could never get a right look at her, he lamented. Sometimes he opened his eyes in time to see the flutter of her gray cloak as she passed out of his door, and once he caught a gleam of red. It was a red hood she wore, not like anything that mortal ever saw before, but just as if a big scarlet tulip had been crushed down over her head with all the leaves sticking out round her face. And his blood always curdled when she gave a cry going over the threshold, as if she was being dragged away into some dreaded torment from which she had had a respite.

"It would break the heart in yer breast to hear it, just for all the worl' like the whine of a dog when there's death aroun'," he would say.

But no one could get him to commit himself as to a theory about the comings and goings of the Wee Woman. Whether he fancied her a friendly denizen of fairyland, or a poor wandering ghost dreeing her purgatory for her own sake or the sake of some one loved and living, the inquisitive people of the bog-side could never learn, yet night after night the hearth was swept, and the stool placed that she might have her rest until dawn broke in a flame of gold and pale chilly green over the hill-tops.

So the ghostly story spread, as such stories will, through the country, finding by turns sympathiser and sceptic alike, who yearned, though fear of the supernatural kept most of them away, for a peep through Jamie's window before the black cock gave the signal. But the young fellows from Glenwherry, daring and mischievous as they were, had made up their minds to solve the mystery, and nothing daunted, holding their breath steadily, they drew close to the little window, and out of the thick blackness of the last night-hour glared into the haunted kitchen.

The firelight flickered fitfully at first, so that their eyes, half blinded with the darkness, saw nothing save shadows; then, suddenly, a gleam shot from the heart of the dying turf, and showed a vision that drove them back from the window, saddened and ashamed.

It was only the old man asleep in his settle-bed, his thin, wrinkled profile outlined like a cameo against the background of dark wood, and the patient old hands, that were so gentle and capable, folded upon his breast, as when he had lain down to sleep.

After that the Wee Gray Woman might come and go, without dread of being watched for, or disturbed, and among the Glenwherry lads Jamie found a set of stalwart partisans, whose judgment in his favour dare not be gainsaid.

He was not altogether devoid of occupation and amusement in his lonely existence. The little one-roomed cabin was tidy as a woman might have kept it. And though he harboured neither cat nor dog, during one winter at least—the severest winter known for many years in that locality—he had a pet, and the pet was a cricket. Imported from a neighbouring fireside, he had trained it with the utmost patience and skill until the diminutive dusty-looking object learned to jump out from behind the big pot in the chimney-corner at his call. The story of his having accomplished such a marvel scarcely gained credence; it was not to be compared to that of his ghostly guest; but the country children cherished it and repeated it in wide-eyed wonder, when they gathered round their elders' knees before the unwelcome bedtime; while the more superstitious asserted that it was the Wee Gray Woman come to bide with Jamie Boyson by day in another guise. It certainly looked uncanny enough, hop-hopping over the floor, chirruping in a shrill, faint treble to his deeper intonation, and, when he lifted it, creeping into the shelter of his hand, as a home bird might that has known and loved and trusted in the kind guardianship.

But once upon a time Jamie Boyson had need of neither ghost nor cricket for company. That was in the days of his early manhood, when, stalwart, supple, and strong, he led the boys of Crebilly to victory on many a hard-fought field of a Sunday, proving himself a champion to be proud of, in throwing the shoulder-stone, and wielding the *camán* against the athletic Glenwherry lads, with big Dan O'Hara at their head. Then, where was his equal to be found at dance or christening? Why, half the girls in the country were in love with him, and hopelessly, too, as they learned to admit to their own sad hearts, that fluttered so uncomfortably under the Sunday 'kerchiefs when he passed, his black head erect, and his shoulders squared like a militia major's, without a look at one of them, up the chapel aisle to his seat next his mother in the old family pew.

The family pew held something else besides his mother; something the very sight of which was enough to bring the red blood in a rush to the roots of his curly dark hair, and make his heart almost leap out of his breast for gladness; something that was small, and fair, and blue-eyed, half-hidden behind his mother's ample form, and scarcely lifting her white lids from the beads she was passing through her fingers.

She was no stranger to him; he had many opportunities of watching her pale sweetness by his own fireside at night, without embarrassing her with that burning gaze of his under the disapproving eyes of all the congregation; but he was wont to say to himself, as a sort of justification that little Rosie at her prayers taught him more about heaven and holiness than the priest could do with all his preaching.

His brother Hugh used to joke him often and often about his fancy for the little orphan girl whom his mother had saved from the poorhouse, and Jamie's brow would glow with the angry red that warned Hugh's tongue to stop, and the laughter to die out of his merry brown face. There were only the two of them left to his mother, and one took little Rosie into his life as a sister, while to the other she, whom the country lads in general had called "a poor, pale wisp o' a thing", became his all, his world, his gateway of Paradise. How the love for her grew up in his heart was a mystery to him. Perhaps it took root when as a little child—the evening she came home to them—she laid her flaxen head on the bashful lad's broad shoulder and would not be parted from him until sleep stole on her unawares and released the tiny hands from their grasp on his strong ones. Or perhaps it came later as he learned to watch delightedly her deft, gentle household ways, and heard her crooning to herself over her flowering, in the rare leisure moments the active, bustling mother allowed.

There was an old song he was very fond of singing about "Lord Edward"—an old song she loved to listen to—and he was always sure of a grateful glance from the shy eyes, when of a winter's night he favoured the little circle around the hearth of Lisnahilt with the stanzas set to an air that was very popular in the district:—

"The day that traitors sold him an' enemies bought him,
The day that the red gold and red blood was paid;
Then the green turned pale and trembled like the dead leaves
*   in autumn.*
An' the heart an' hope of Ireland in the cold grave was laid.

"The day I saw you first, with the sunshine fallin' round ye,
My heart fairly opened with the grandeur of the view;
For ten thousand Irish boys that day did surround ye,
An' I swore to stand by them till death, an' fight for you.

"Ye wor the bravest gentleman an' the best that ever stood,
An' yer eyelids never trembled for danger nor for dread,
An' nobleness was flowin' in each stream of your blood—
My blessin' on ye day and night, an' Glory be your bed.

"My black and bitter curse on the head an' heart an' hand
That plotted, wished, an' worked the fall of this Irish hero bold,
God's curse upon the Irishman that sould his native land,
And hell consume to dust the hand that held the traitor's gold."

Sometimes tired with the day's hard work, she would rest her head against the wall with a low sigh of weariness. She must often be tired, he thought; those little feet had run about so nimbly since early morning, and the little red hands had washed and baked, without a moment's pause; but, please God, that would be all ended soon, when his wife should reign over a home of her own, and he had taken her into the shelter of his strong arms for evermore.

Yet no word of this crossed his lips, though the desire that filled his heart beat like a strong ceaseless wave within his breast, giving him an almost unbearable pain, and he never dreamt but that she knew. In the very effort to control himself, his voice was, curiously, harsh when he spoke to her; and while the poor child trembled at the rude accents, her faltering reply aroused in the big, tender-hearted fellow a wild feeling that was half exquisite pity, and half hate. Ah! if he had only spoken then, the grim tragedy of his life might have been spared him.

One bleak night in autumn a sound outside drew him to the door, and opening it, he stood listening.

"John Conan's calves are in the clover-field," he said; "go and put them out."

Rose lifted her timid blue eyes to him questioningly.

"Do you hear me?" he asked.

"But I'm afraid," she murmured; "it's so dark, an'—"

He pointed his finger to the open door and the black stormy night outside.

"Go," he repeated fiercely, turning to his chair, and lifting his pipe off the shelf, and the girl passed into the darkness without another word.

What madness was on him that he had spoken to the little girl, and sent her on such an errand? he asked himself when she had gone. He had been conscious of a strange, sore sensation all day, since at Crebilly Fair, that forenoon, Tom M'Mullan had proposed a match between her and his son Jack, one of the wildest young scamps in the whole countryside, and the unreasoning jealousy grew and grew until he had wreaked his pain in vengeance on his poor Rosie's unoffending head.

"Oh! amn't I the queer, ungrateful fool," he muttered, "to trate the wee lass this way."

An hour passed, he waiting every moment to hear her footfall on the threshold, and his mother speculating comfortably that she had gone in for a gossip to John Conan's. At last he could bear his regret and the suspense no longer, and went out to seek her.

It was only a step or two to the clover-field, and reaching the low stone wall he called to her eagerly in the darkness. The startled calves, still enjoying their forbidden banquet, lowed back in answer.

He vaulted the gate, every step of the way familiar to him by night as by noon, and called anxiously and long. Then he remembered his mother's surmise, and turned across the field to Conan's.

There was no little Rosie sitting with the laughing girls grouped together in the corner, over a quilting frame, and in response to his husky demand a couple of Conan's young sons volunteered to accompany him on his search—Hugh, his brother, being away for the night in a market town many miles off.

He walked on, quickly, in the direction of the bog, guided only by his intimate knowledge of the treacherous path that wound like a serpent across the marshy windswept surface. He heard the small waves beat against each other with a faint sad sound, while overhead not one solitary star glimmered, to light his heart with hopefulness. Through the terrible night, and into the dawn, his frantic search continued, calling her name in a hoarse agony that wrung the souls of those who heard him.

"Rosie, Rosie, my little girl, it's Jamie's callin'. Ah! come, can't ye, an' don't be hidin' there. Don't ye hear me darlin', it's Jamie, an' the supper's waitin' on us. Let Conan's calves go—they're always a trouble to somebody, but *you* come home. Here, take my han' "—stretching out his arms into the empty shadows—"take it, love, an' don't be afeard, nothin' can touch ye, pulse o' my heart, when I'm beside ye, Rosie! Rosie!"

And so on through the dreary hours, over the wild bogland, his voice rang in pitiful entreaty, until jagged streaks of golden red flamed like trailing banners in the East, and the birds, wide-awake, took up in a chorus, clear-tongued and grateful, the morning song; but alas! for him, whose song-bird had flown afar, and for whom the dawn henceforth should hold no radiance, nor the rose-flushed mellow evening any passion.

Yet his frantic cry broke in upon the happy choir, and the blackbird and thrush, from hedge and beechentree, watched him staggering home in the sunshine, murmuring through lips that scarcely knew the words they uttered—"Rosie, Rosie, girl dear, come home."

Some hours later a turf-cutter, crossing the burn to his work, caught a gleam of something bright under the cold running water. It was little Rosie's fair head lying against the stones in the shade of the drooping sallytrees, whither through the darkness, blinded by her sorrow, she had wandered to her death.

Jamie Boyson aged suddenly after that. When the friends of his boyhood had grown into sturdy, middle-aged men, strong and hearty, he was already old, with a gloom upon him that no smile was ever known to lighten. In time, when his mother died, and Hugh had married, he grew unable to bear the sound of children's chatter through the rooms where he had once hoped to see his own little ones at play, and came to live his life alone in the cabin by the burnside, from whence he could watch the very spot where poor Rosie's gentle head had lain under the clear cold ripples.

So the country folk, noting his absent dim blue eyes, and wandering talk about the Wee Gray Woman, grew to believe that it was little Rosie's ghost come to bear him company until the call should sound for him, and his broken and desolate heart should find peace.

That was many, many years ago; and, perhaps, they have met long since in heaven, where Jamie Boyson, young, and straight, and strong again, with all the bitterness gone from his heart, has taken little Rosie in his arms and told her the truth at last.

The Blanket Fiend

Beatrice Grimshaw

There is secret bread in the wilderness and on the edges of the world. That thunderous green evening I was eating mine; it may have looked like camp biscuit, but it was far other and more precious. For it, I had paid down love, youth, strength, home and friends. Worth all this? I do not know. Ask the opium-eater if his little ball of dreams is worth all that it has cost him. Whatever the answer may be, he will hold to the ball and the magic in it.

So I ate my biscuits and looked down, in the last light of day, upon the tangle of valleys, like the spreading fingers of a hand, that I had reached that afternoon. And the secret bread was very sweet in my mouth, because, once again, I had conquered the unknown. No white man before me had seen these valleys, or climbed the enormous, nightmare slopes that led to them; slopes on which my carriers and I had endlessly laboured, enchanted to one spot, like ants that climb and slip upon a marble wall. But at long last we had conquered; the days were over, and the weeks that went before them, and we saw what no man save the wild head-hunters of the ranges had seen—the deadly river talked of away down the coasts; whispered about of nights round the smudge fires of camp, when mosquitoes whined and the murder-bird cried in the bush; laughed at in merry daylight, but cringingly believed in under night—the river that was called in a score of dialects, a dozen different languages, "Wicked".

Between tribes who killed each other at sight, over places all but unclimbable, through the air it seemed, or on the wings of the streaming south-east trade, the stories about that river passed, somehow. On the "Cape of Good Hope" that is the nose of Northern New Guinea, in the great prison Bay of Humboldt, on upper mysterious reaches of the warlike Sepik, they told you about Wicked River. Not men lived in that valley, but devils. No such devils were ever seen or heard of elsewhere. They caught you in a dusky fog, and the fog turned to living wings and bore you down to hell. They made horrible noises, and when you heard the noise, your bones melted away inside your skin, and you sank down, poured out like water, and so ended . . .

There were white traders on the coasts who had heard these tales; their story coincided with those that I had gleaned among the natives, but they believed none of it. It was "nigger nonsense", "yarns invented by travellers to make themselves look big", and, as a last, damning comment, it was "koi-koi", the untranslatable native term which includes every kind of hoax or lie.

So, when I went off the deep end, with a handful of carriers and very few stores (but that was all I could afford), I said I was going to look for gold. Otherwise, I think, they would have kept and bound me, as one mad.

But I knew what I knew. I had paid enough for knowing. And one piece of knowledge was, that there is never quite nothing in a native tale. What about the devil pig of Mount Victoria? What about blue "sorcerer-lights" that danced where oil has now been found? What about the Papuan tree-climbing alligator, in which no one believed until someone, recently, found dragons on the Malayan isle of Komodo? I could go on till you were tired . . .

It had been told me, and I believed, that the Wicked Valley and River were found over the top of an "unclimbable" mountain, which, if you did succeed in climbing it, gave you a view of five rivers like the fingers of a hand, all running into one. There were the fivefold rivers, there was the valley; and the sun, that night, was going down upon a view of fine meadows, chines and slopes and coppices, meant by Nature for the growing of banana, sugar-cane, great sweet potatoes, giant taro . . . But in the valley, along the whole of one side, and that the richest by far, there had not been a tree cleared away; no burn-off, no digging or preparing soil. The other side was rocky cliff, unusable.

I had had my doubts before, they vanished at that spectacle. For in the distance, touched by one finger-tip of sinking sun, I could see the little brown shapes of a mountain village, like fungus clinging to rock. That the folk of the village should leave such a valley untouched, argued for the truth of all I had been told.

I had an interpreter with me, a man who knew English and something of two or three hill languages. I was minded to march upon the village next day, make friends with the people, if that might be, before they had the chance to attack us, and afterwards, sure of my ground, investigate the valley. Now that I had arrived I was mad to get into it, but I knew that I should be mad in another sense if I did not first make sure of the people. They roll rocks on your head in the inland mountains, and they do it very well from their point of view, which, naturally, is not yours.

Quite sure that I should find myself alone, I turned out early next morning from my tent, and stepped across the few feet that separated me from the carriers' fly. I was scarce round the other side when I saw a procession of from sixty to eighty men winding across the nearest slope, dim as ghosts in the dawn. The valley was full of mist; as I watched, light, boiling up from the lands below, frothed over into the far end of the valley and showed, for a moment, a deep, dark pool in the river.

Then I perceived the warriors on the other side of the valley ranging themselves above that point and coming to a halt. They were a long way off, but the concerted shout they raised rang so clearly as to wake my carriers out of sleep, and set them fumbling nervously for the loaded rifles that were always within reach.

"Hold on," I ordered, "don't fire." For I wanted, above all things, to be friends with these people.

The sun was up a bit now, and I could see the mountaineers plainly, standing on the extreme verge of the precipice. They seemed, with their fluttering crests of cockatoo feathers, their bristling spears, and the unstable, poised look of their bodies, like a covey of strange birds just about to take flight. I should not have been surprised if they had spread wings and planed away across the valley.

Instead of that, they parted right and left, there on the edge of the cliff, and two men, stepping from behind, swung out across the cliff, like children playing "honey-pots", something big, brown-pinkish and screaming . . .

I felt as I felt once in the War, when an army mule lunged out and kicked me in the chest. That was for a moment. In the next moment I saw that the screaming creature had four legs. They swung it solemnly several times and then let go. It went down, into the mist, turning over and over. I heard it scream again as it struck bottom, and then there was silence.

For some few minutes the file of Papuans stood motionless, save for the wimpling of their head feathers in the breeze; and I will swear that every man of them had his toes right over the edge. It made me giddy to look at them.

Then the white fog below them changed swiftly to red, and the sun came up sliding behind a hill, very quickly, like the pushed-up sun in a theatre. The warriors melted. In another moment they were running hell-for-leather up a height of one in three, heading for my camp. They had the air of men who say, "Business is done, now for pleasure." And they shook their seven-foot bows and leaped a bit, whoo-whooping loud, like hounds. Exactly like . . . for exactly the same reasons.

Now I wish I had time to tell, and you had time to listen, about my making friends with these wild things, as I had done in similar tight places more than once, as I shall do, please the Red Gods, another time or two before that day arrives when the gamble with life goes the wrong way, and my stake, so often hazarded, is lost. But you are not of the wilderness; you have no patience. So you must know just this—that by night-time, I and my carriers were sitting among the men of Wicked River, fed with tit-bits by their hands, caressed, adorned, almost cried over.

They were splendid creatures, with naked chests like barrels, and legs sheer bunches of muscle; their shoulders would have wedged tight in any ship's cabin door, and their black, deep-buried eyes scintillated when they spoke with fires unknown to civilised men. I found myself hoping that civilisation might never find these magnificent, untouched creatures. What could it give better than that they had?

They took me for a god from heaven, as untouched mountain people generally do. But there was something in their way of receiving me that puzzled me a little. For they were not surprised by my white skin quite as other tribes had been. They seemed, in their own odd way, to know something about me. The interpreter was little use, and my own scraps of coast language did not carry me far; still, I judged that the finest of the men, a village head-man, was pleased that I had come, and thought I might do him some service.

He took me by both hands again and again, chattering loudly and repeating his words, so that I might wake up to understanding—just as John Bull is wont to do on a holiday trip to Boulogne. I have his picture clearly in my mind as we sat all together on the ground in that high camp, with the sun going down again, and the remains of a handsome feast of pig and potato, white baked yam and crayfish, scattered about for the women to pick up by and by when we were gone. The air was golden glass, and the hill peaks had a bloom on them like purple damsons ripe to fall; but farther off, they climbed up, chalcedony blue; and no man owned or knew them. The headman's face was like a coin against it all, profile of copper, nobly traced. I saw in it the sudden liking that blooms in these tropic hearts, liking for me, and trust—he who had been eager for my dangling head an hour or so before. And with it all a sort of terror.

"He is afraid of something," I thought. "He wants me to deliver him from his fear." I realised how strong and immortal I must seem to him; how powerful to aid, as our gods seem to us. "If he thinks well to grant it . . . !" was in the head-man's burning, bison eyes, fixed anxiously on me. He was taking bracelets from his arm now; the twice coiled tusk of a great pig; twists of red seeds with little black eyes in them. He was offering these . . .

It is strange how you may catch yourself suddenly in another's eyes. One does not think of one's appearance, till one sees it, mirrored there. I had forgotten I was six feet three, blue eyes, with yellowy hair, long untrimmed. I remembered it then, because I saw the head-man was thinking of my looks, judging me by them. In another minute I saw the reason.

A girl, very slowly, but not, I thought, timidly, came out from behind the mass of warriors and stood beside the head-man, not far from the carriers and from me. And when I saw her it was my turn to be surprised. She was naked, native, savage, but she was part white.

I don't say she was not well-looking. Her nose and lips had escaped flatness; her hair was Papuan hair, an immense, teased, floating bush, but it was brown, not black, and it had lights in it that made it look like the expanded feathers of a bird. As for her figure, she being a native girl and young, it was naturally perfect. Her colour, fully displayed by the mountain "dress"—which is a piece of decorated string, no more—was a not unpleasing deep amber.

Of course, I tried her in pidgin English, but she merely shook her head. I saw by her ornaments and her uncut hair that she was unwedded. And it became plain, in another minute or two, that the head-man (whom I had mentally nicknamed "Georgy", because he looked jolly and capable, and just a bit sly—like a certain statesman we all know) had something very important to say about her.

I cursed my luck and the stupidity of my interpreter, who didn't know more than three or four dialects, little more than I knew myself, and hadn't hit it off with anyone. What could "Georgy" be up to? Offering me the girl as a bride? That might be, since they seemed to have some inexplicable strain of white in the tribe and, what was more, to value it, which was by no means usual. But even if he were offering her, that was not all. There was something of more importance afoot than the mere disposal of a girl.

Bagi-Bagi, the interpreter, only increased my perplexity by the stray words caught here and there. He translated haltingly, almost weeping over his inability to understand more.

"He say—he say—he say—Bad. Very bad. He, say—he say—he say—he say—Sky. Good."

"Oh," I shouted of a sudden, "he's saying things are bad up here, and it's well there are angels from heaven come along . . . Go to it, Bagi-Bagi; you're beginning to catch on."

There followed an interlude of rattling speech that sounded as if it had been shot from a machine-gun. Bagi-Bagi gave up in despair. But it was I who was catching on now; I captured a significant word or two, many times repeated as if for emphasis. "Georgy", it seemed, was telling me that if I could handle a certain job that nobody else could tackle, nothing would be too good for me. Bracelets. Yams. Pigs. Potatoes. Girls. (In the plural, the elaborate multi-plural, if my knowledge of dialect was not running away with me.) And something that seemed to mean times of year, seasons, stars—I could not make that out at all.

But I nodded my head a great many times, told "Georgy", gravely, in English, that he was a fine old fighting cock, and that I would do my best to oblige him, whatever it might be. I think he gathered my meaning. He turned off the tap of his eloquence, said something brief and commanding to the girl, and, with his followers, settled down for a happy evening.

The girl melted away, and I didn't think any more about her till she came back, with twenty or thirty others and a number of young men carrying mantles of bark cloth.

"This is going to be a dance," I said to Bagi-Bagi somewhat wearily, for I had seen a hundred and half a hundred more, in years gone by, and was by no means anxious to sit through another.

"By Scott, sir, it is," he answered readily. (Bagi-Bagi was nothing if not idiomatic.) "I very bucked, I think they dance all the (embroidered) night." But they did not; whereby both of us were disappointed, and only one disagreeably. The dance was very significant, very wonderful and astonishingly short.

After some of the usual preliminary caperings, the men and the girls formed into two opposite ranks. The former, holding high their bark cloth mantles, and dancing tip-toe with amazing lightness, approached the girls, who fled, dancing all the time, but acting terror effectively. Along the verge of the cliff, in the light of the torches and the fires, they danced, towards a space of reed-grass, eight or ten feet high. Here there was semi-darkness; the lights of the flames just showed the last and most astounding figure of the dance, wherein each man flung his enormous mantle over a girl, fought with her for a moment, and then—just as I was anticipating the usual, commonplace, love-struggle—danced back, completely alone. The girls had vanished under the mantles, as a conjuror's rabbit vanishes under his handkerchief. The mantles, after a moment, were picked up by their owners, flaccid and empty.

By and by the girls reappeared from behind us, mysteriously, danced a little more and departed. I saw the amber girl was crying, but I was too much obsessed by the dance to notice her particularly. Of course the high, dusky reed-grass had helped in the disappearing trick, but it was all immensely effective, and I clapped with vigour. Then I began to wonder—what did it all mean? Native dances are never meaningless. Was it possible that this was a representation of the mystery I had come to solve? . . .

The girls passed by. The amber girl had stopped crying; she stared at me as she passed, her eyes big with feeling. I nodded to her and went on thinking.

It was then that I felt, as the solitary explorer does at times feel most bitterly, the want of a white man to talk to. There's much to be said for journeying alone, and much against. On the latter side, the impossibility of discussing plans is perhaps the heaviest count.

I was bursting with the thought that had come to me; and yet I could not say for certain whether I was a fool to entertain it or no. When you are infinitely wiser than anyone within sight; when you are being obeyed as a father, honoured as a god, it is hard sometimes to keep your balance, and remember that you are, after all, only a very ordinary sort of ass.

I think that Bagi-Bagi, who was used to the ways of white men, guessed something of this. When the dance was over and the head-man, with much back-slapping and grinning, and many incomprehensible signs as to what we were all going to do on the morrow, had disappeared, Bagi-Bagi, on soundless bare feet, came up to where I sat alone. I was smiling as I thought. That is a trick, and a good one, that I learned from books—never let your followers see you down-hearted.

Perhaps he guessed. "Sir," he suggested, "more better you talkem along me. More better you spittem out everyfing all same beach-de-mar."

I remembered the look of a *bêche-de-mer* in sea shallows, turning itself hideously inside out because somebody had looked at it, and I burst out laughing.

"Well, Bagi-Bagi," I said, "I think I know what's the matter here, but I can't believe it."

"E!"

"You see, Bagi-Bagi—you know what a Chinaman is?"

"Me savvy Sinaman all right. Plenty stop salt walter."

"Well, in the Chinaman's country, ever so long ago, a big white chief travelling found a valley like this and there was a bad devil in a river. It was in a place a long way from anywhere, that they called Lu Tzu Chiang. The white chief was in a great hurry to get home and talk about where he had been, so he didn't try to look up the devil, he just heard what they had to tell him, and said it wasn't true, and went away. But I think he must have believed some of it, for he put it in a book. And then everybody died or grew old, and nobody went there any more, and all the world forgot about the devil. But I have the book and I've read it, and I'm damned, Bagi-Bagi, if the same devil hasn't turned up here."

Bagi-Bagi, squatting like a monkey at my feet and solemnly chewing betel-nut, turned the quid in his cheek before he answered.

"I think, sir," he said presently, with a lick at his lime spatula, "I think you-me go see."

※

The valley, in morning light, was even more beautiful than I had thought. From the summit of the cliffs one could see its opulent green slopes and the furry tops of its thickets; but it was only on near approach that fern-trees like parasols of finest lace; pawpaw, that lovely little palm with golden fruit and ivory flowers; bamboo; begonia; flowers the shape and colour of orange candles, set out on ropes of green; flowers like amethyst goblets, growing bare on the ground, became clearly visible. A mountain paradise, yet silent and lonesome, somewhat strange, for all its sweetness of flower and of fruit, not friendly . . .

Bagi-Bagi and I had climbed all the way down from the top alone; the carriers would not go within a bow-shot of the brink, and our mountain friends had not yet appeared. That was all to the good, so far as I was concerned. I wanted to investigate, unhampered.

Bagi-Bagi was not the man to stop me; curiosity was at once his virtue and his vice. But I thought he liked the unfriendliness of the valley no more than I did; understood it better, perhaps. It was he who nailed it down with a name.

"Sir," he remarked, standing up very straight, with his feet dark brown among the fallen yellow pawpaw fruits, and his coppery thin body outlined against a bush of jasmine, "Sir, this place be too blanky quiet; he no talk."

It was true. Down here in the belly of the hills, there was no wind to ruffle the rich grasses, no stir among the fern-trees and bamboo, that are the greatest whisperers of all the mountain woods. The river, fed by its five thin streams, was oddly silent. Its width may have been about fifty yards on an average, save where it opened out into a longish shallow or pool, and there it was somewhat wider. In the midst of the shallow there was, not quite a ripple, but a stir, a breathing of the black water.

"That's where the ford will be," I thought. "These mountain men are poor swimmers; that is the place where they would naturally cross to get at the garden land on the other side. If they ever did cross. I see no gardens, but there's certainly something like a track. On one side only . . . Queer."

The sunshine, thick as honey, filled the place. You could almost hear the exultant singing of the light sky. Red dragon-flies, like shards of living coral, planed above the candle flowers. "They do not care whether one lives or dies," I found myself thinking. "*It* does not care." Long I had known that nameless power that walks in the wilderness, godless, incurious, magnificently apart. Was not my secret bread the very shewbread of its altar? There are some who will understand.

With an effort I shook myself free of dreams, walked forward, Bagi-Bagi following cautiously some distance behind. Yes, there was a track that led towards the shallow; towards it, not all the way. It stopped short, oddly, some feet clear of the river bank.

I paused here and thought hard. I remembered the wild tale of the Victorian traveller, Baber; the fiend that inhabited the river ford in unknown China. Could it be true that such a thing existed? Or was the coincidence of two similar tales due only to the presence of a few stray Chinamen upon the coast, who had brought with them some of their native legends?

But there are strange creatures in the world's dark places; survivals, it may be, of an earlier day. Who knows but a living dinosaur may yet be found? Who has pierced to its depths the mystery of the Australian bunyip?

These things were in my mind as I stood, motionless, in the hot still valley, with the last few feet of the track untraversed before me, and just beyond the end of the track, below a fringe of reed-grass and tree ferns, the ford that was talked of from main range to coast-line, from wild head-hunter tribes to poaching, sly Chinese. Lies, all lies, the white traders had said . . . and yet—

Under ordinary circumstances, that ford should have been trampled like a cattle-yard, on both sides of the river. It was the only way from the rocky side where I stood, to those rich agricultural lands just opposite, the natural food gardens of the village behind me—and, let me tell you, the inland Papuan does not value good garden lands lightly. They are his bank, his gold-mine.

Yet the village had never touched, would never touch that land. All its food was obtained from the inferior gardens, miles away, that I had glimpsed in the distance, coming up. No wonder "Georgy", that good-humoured savage with the sly, clever eyes, had promised me girls and potatoes and pig-tusk bracelets by the score if I, the strange chief descended from the skies, proved powerful and kind enough to deliver the place from its terror. No wonder he had done his little best, throwing precious live pigs and other things from the crown of the precipice, to placate the monster . . .

Other things? I found myself dwelling upon the words. What had put that in my head? I had seen a pig thrown, no more.

Old days, near twenty years ago, came back in a rush. The Papuan side, before the coasts were civilised. The Western rivers, stately processions up and down the Bamu, Turama,

Purari, that I had seen and marvelled over; bands of fighting men, armed and plumed, singing loud brassy songs, as they ferried along a decorated canoe with sometimes a dead pig upon it, sometimes a dead man. The secret talk among cannibal tribes, in which pig and man were words almost interchangeable; a certain tendency to look upon the two as coins of different value, meet for transactions with the spiritual world.

. . . Why was the half-white girl crying last night after the dance? Why did she fix those strange grey-amber eyes of hers on you so anxiously? Fool—you thought it was because she admired your height and your yellow tousled head! It was nothing of the kind. She knew what was waiting for her and feared it. She saw that you were strong and hoped . . .

"Bagi-Bagi," I said, turning round to speak to the interpreter, "what do they think of white people here? How did that girl get her colour? Down on the coast they usually kill half-castes."

"True, sir. True they kill them. This feofle another kind. He don't know white man." (Oh, bitter, unconscious sarcasm!) "I telling you, sir, you-me we seen everything, not like these dam cannibals. You-me we know about airaflanes. Sir, bee-fore Englisman take this place, one time Siamani man come along in airyflane, flied over. One village he stop, one night. Beehind, he go. This girl's mother, she have her piccaninny, she die. Piccaninny half white. Belong one great devil-devil, this feofle say, devil living in the sky. Sir, they think a dam lot of this girl, thass what for they pay you with her, if you taking away the devil along river."

"Yes, yes, but what will they do with her if I can't manage the job?"

"Then, sir, they frow her all same they frow that fig. Fig no good, try another thing, try devil-devil girl."

I had known it. I had known—seen!—worse things than that. Yet the golden valley seemed to turn grey as I heard; the river, creeping among the flowers and ferns like a long black leech in a swamp, became suddenly horrible to me.

"Bagi-Bagi," I said, and I heard myself grinding my teeth as I spoke, "if I wait here a year, this thing, whatever it is, dies, or else I do."

"Me," declared Bagi-Bagi scornfully—yet I saw that he was edging away from the river, "me, I don' believe nothing stop."

We were both standing with our backs to the black river and our faces to the little mushroom houses high on the cliff. I think I was looking for the girl; I don't know what he was looking for. But while we stood there, something occurred behind us that made me swing round in my tracks as if worked by a machine. As for Bagi-Bagi, he yelled and ran.

It was merely a sound—but what a sound! If one had ripped out, in one piece, the deck of a sizeable cutter, and flung it violently upon the surface of the sea, the noise might have been something like what I heard.

I was just too late to see what had caused it. But the whole surface of the ford, that had been smooth and shining as black onyx, was ruffled into tiny cross waves, pitching and foaming like the breakers in an ocean storm, and the reeds by the margin swayed as if an invisible hand was shaking them.

Nothing more happened, though I waited so long that Bagi-Bagi had time to scramble half-way up the cliff, think better of it and slowly, uncertainly, come back. The valley relapsed into silence, so heavy that we could hear the hum of the red dragon-flies and the faint, papery rustle of some small, creeping thing that moved among the reeds. Slowly, the exultation that had held me so long, the curious, malicious joy at being out of reach, right over the edge of the world, died away. And in its place I knew the nightmare despair that is the other side of that glittering shield. I felt myself dead and done for, wandering in a world of shades . . .

If it is not good for man to be alone in an ordinary world of passing people; it is, still less, good for him to encounter the blinding solitudes, the aloneness, so cold that it burns while it freezes, of the world's far edge. Yet one will pay that, and pay again, for the sake of the strange joys and the bread that has enchantment in it.

I suppose all these things were in my mind as I climbed the side of the steep gorge, half mechanically. I suppose I was thinking, too, of the horrible, mysterious thing I had heard, but not seen, planning what my next move must be. But I do not remember anything about that, because of what happened when I reached the top of the cliff.

There was a patch of timber there, some tall fir trees, shaped like trees in an old-fashioned "farmyard" box of toys, a cedar or so, a clump of shiny things like laurustinus. The trunks of the firs and cedars and the low bushiness of the smaller trees hid the top of the cliff from the village. I had just set my foot upon the level, when something darted out at me from among the brushwood and seized me by the legs.

With the monster of the ford haunting my brain, I had almost fired off the revolver which all New Guinea explorers keep in their belts. It was lucky that I did not, for the next moment showed me that the thing which clung about me and held me fast was no wild beast. It was the amber girl.

She had been newly decorated after a fashion familiar to me, and significant. Shell beads, white dogs' teeth, feathers, scarlet and black seeds, had been tied into her hair and wreathed about her neck and arms. Her cheeks and her bosom were rouged with the red paint found in the pods of a mountain bean. In fine, she was decked for marriage.

But—even a native girl, I knew, to whom marriage brings no romance, does not meet her change in life with the sobs and cries that were now being uttered by the amber maid. She crouched at my feet, rebellious, terrified, defying the tradition of her people in a manner that would have seemed nothing short of blasphemous to the village women had they seen her. It did not astonish me; I and Bagi-Bagi knew that—the supposed supernatural love which had given her birth, had in truth moulded her very differently from the meek, black, bare creatures who were her ordinary mates.

Nevertheless, I was taken aback. Because it seemed as if the very idea of being given to me was producing this frantic terror and dismay.

Now you may be as far as possible from wanting to marry, permanently or temporarily, a young thing with the shape of an Oread, a skin like golden bronze and no clothes at all, but if you are human you will not be flattered to discover that she shares your point of view. I was inclined to call the girl a silly little idiot. But she wouldn't have understood me anyhow. So I acted in the best classical tradition, raised her off her knees and set her upright, loosened her clutching hands (they were pretty, but a mass of wet red paint) and said something or other in a soothing tone.

It had no effect at all. She pointed to the valley, far below, with the black snake of the river slipping through, clapped her palms together sharply, and shook her head with violence.

Bagi-Bagi, who had waited at the top for me, and was now squatting unconcernedly on his hams, licking his eternal betel-nut spatula, remarked:

"Sir, I think she very dam disappoint you no kill that thing."

"Wait till I see it," was my answer. A plan had suddenly arisen in my mind; perhaps the sight of clutching, painted hands, half-white, of grey-amber eyes dropping tears, had given my straining mind the one last impetus it needed.

"What's she worrying over besides that?" I asked. "You needn't tell me that's all." The girl, silent for a moment, had broken forth again. Her weeping was terrible to see.

"Sir, lass night the night before full moon, thass why."

"Well, what in the name of—"

"Sir, full moon proper time for try something. Lass night close up full, them feofle they frow one fig. To-night, suppose you can't do nothing, sir, they frow girl. They no wait. Girl she tellem me, she makem talk with her hand."

The amber girl had managed then to communicate clearly with Bagi-Bagi, by means of sign language, in which the savage woman is always more proficient than the man.

"I don't see," I objected, "why they make such a fuss about the thing anyhow. Can't they keep out of its way?"

"All-a-time," said Bagi-Bagi succinctly, "him live along big water, sometime him live along small water. Sometime woman she go get water, debil-debil catchem woman. All garden belong feofle he no good now, want this good garden, can't get him. By and by very hungerry-hungerry."

Yes, they had reason enough, this little isolated tribe, whose food gardens were almost used up, whose women were taken and devoured (but I added a grain of salt to that)—reason full and plenty, according to their standards, for sacrificing the amber girl, daughter of gods, and possession most precious. She knew it. She looked at me with the eyes of a hunted wallaby, than which there is nothing more piteous, and pawed me with her little painted hands.

She had reason to, more than she knew or could have understood had I talked an hour. For I was suffering at that moment the greatest temptation of my life, and she was concerned in it.

No, not what you think. Something much less commonplace, less easily dealt with. You must remember I was an explorer, and one from whom, hitherto, the laurels of success had been withheld. Not, I may say, because I had done nothing to deserve them—I had won medals and fellowships a dozen times, so far as good and original work goes, which isn't very far, after all. But I had done nothing spectacular; I hadn't got lost and been rescued, or lost and found somebody else; I hadn't been captured by cannibals, I hadn't discovered purple cows or yellow dragons anywhere . . .

Now, I thought, there was the most brilliant chance that had ever befallen man, waiting for me down in that valley, if my conjectures were right, and if I could only do as I wished and not, perhaps, as I ought.

The fiend of the ford could – in my judgment—be one of three things only. It might be a legend, an obsession of terror, that had no actual base in fact. That was what most folk would have thought. Baber and his contemporaries waved away the Chinese fiend in just that fashion, and I have not heard that anyone has ever tried to prove or disprove their verdict.

Or—it might be a previously unknown variety of sting-ray, such as are common in the seas about New Guinea, a giant freshwater-ray, with the ray habit of flinging itself into the air, and driving down whatever happens to be in the way. Good enough for a certain amount of glory if I discovered, and proved, that.

Or—but I hardly allowed myself to think of the third possibility. It was just as exciting, should it prove true, as the Piltdown skull, and the Java tailed man, and might prove or disprove just as much—if . . .

I had dynamite with me; I could use it, and it would certainly be successful. One could not miss with dynamite. I had also some thin iron bars, meant for trading, that could be hammered into big shark-hooks, strong enough, with a line of lawyer-cane, to hold the Great Sea-Serpent himself. I inclined very much to the hook and line business, because

I knew that if the devil proved to be a ray, one was as good as another, but if it was what I hardly dared to hope, the use of dynamite would be fatal to my chance.

So—I had to choose between the eighty per cent chance of the hook and line, and the hundred per cent. chance of the dynamite—which last would, incidentally, beggar me of the finest opportunity man ever . . . I said that before, I beg your pardon. The very memory of it excites me beyond all—

To get back. I told Bagi-Bagi to go and fetch the iron bars and a good length of cane. Also a couple of stones for hammer and anvil; to bring them down to the riverside where I would wait. And I began climbing down again . . . As I went I shouted, on an afterthought, "Bring the dynamite."

The amber girl came with me. It was Rupert Brooke, I think, who said, "*There's wisdom in women, of more than they have known.*" He was right. That girl was a savage, except for the little trace she may have kept of half-white heredity; yet she guessed instantly at what was in my mind, understood me, as a dog understands, without the necessity of translating thought into words. She knew that the balance of safety, of certainty rather, was falling in the wrong direction, and she would not leave me, any more than a dog will leave you if he suspects you of intent to desert him.

She stayed with me as I climbed down to the river flat again, followed after a long interval by Bagi-Bagi, who had brought with him the iron bars, a file, a length of cane, the stones and a firestick; also the plug of dynamite and a fuse . . .

She sat on her heels like a little wooden image of the kind the northern Papuans perch on house-tops, watching. Her tears had ceased; she was saving them until she knew whether they were going to be needed or not.

It took Bagi-Bagi and myself a long time to heat the iron and hammer it into shape with our primitive tools. She never moved. The sun sank down towards the ranges and struck fire into the dusky pool. Once, when I went to look at it, I thought I saw the whole under-surface stirring, as if the water had suddenly come alive.

The girl watched me, and said nothing.

"Gad," I thought, "the white blood in you tells. You've pluck, and you can hold your tongue." She looked at me with those strange grey-amber eyes of hers, and I swear you could see the white soul of her coming up and unfolding, as a lily rises and opens in a lake.

I went back and hammered at my iron. I did not know—yet—whether I was going to use it or not.

It was done, and I grasped in my hand a hook and line that would be powerful enough to hold anything on earth or under water. Only remained to find a bird or some small animal, secure it, living, to the hook, and make one's trial.

In the other hand I held the plug of dynamite with the fuse cut short and inserted. And which of the two I was going to use I could not for the life of me decide.

The dynamite would assuredly make all things safe; so safe that there would be no evidence left for me to carry back. The hook might, probably would, catch the monster and, in any circumstances, leave me enough to swear by. But it was not a certainty. One might miss—and then?

If there had been plenty of time . . . but that was just what there was not. Our rough amateur blacksmithing had taken too long. I could not try both plans, fish for an hour or two and then, if unsuccessful, use the dynamite. I had thought of that, earlier. Now, with the afternoon beginning to darken, with, swift sunset very near and the night of the full moon almost upon me, I knew that I must decide quickly. Which was it to be? The chance of fame, that through my life had eluded me, or immediate and certain sacrifice of it all?

I don't pretend to be more high-minded than my neighbours. I do not know what I should have done, though I think I can guess, if the deciding factor had not suddenly appeared in the shape of a wallaby.

The creature, brown and furry, a kangaroo in all but size, came bounding down the scarps of the cliff, as if pursued by some enemy. I heard the villagers coming, and guessed that it was flying from them. It took no account of Bagi-Bagi or the girl or myself. It went past us in a series of amazing leaps, making for what must long have been the wild things' sanctuary—the land beyond the river. From the low bank it leapt off, in a tremendous bound that should have carried it across, but did not, because, at the critical moment, a booming shout came down from the top of the cliff, ter- rifying the already terrified creature and making it swerve.

It fell with a splash right into the middle of the pool. And as it fell there rose, out of the water, something enormous, black, blanket-shaped, of indeterminate outline, a thing more like some maniac's half-formed idea of a fish flung out of the world of thought before it had time fully to materialize than anything else one could conceive. It was not natural, therein lay the horror.

The wallaby screamed, a cry like the cry of a child, suddenly stifled. For the huge thing, wrapping itself in an instant about the frantic creature, simply abolished its existence. The first white ray of full moon looking over the top of the ridge, fell on the monster as it quietly and without disturbance, sank.

Then the amber girl opened her mouth and screamed as the little wallaby had screamed when falling. And I gave myself no more time to think, for the knowledge that was on me now tempted, scorched like fire. I cut the fuse an inch shorter, lit it, and flung the plug into the pool. It exploded with a dull crash, and the cliffs echoed back the sound.

A black bubble the size of a bell-tent shot up, weltered for a moment in the mingling rays of sunset and full moon, and then dissolved. The pool was filled with floating bits like blots of ink. I was half mad with the thought of what I had done; I flung myself half over the edge, and reached for some of the pieces. They came up, masses of dark jelly that slid through my fingers. "I might have kept parts—I could have waited—photographed," I thought. "But it's gone!"

Behind me the shout broke forth again, much nearer. The warriors were coming down the cliff. They had seen.

"Georgy" was at their head. It is frightful to remember how he hugged and embraced me. I understood him to say that not only the amber girl but all the girls in the place were mine, if I chose, and that as for pigs, I had only to name my fancy. I was almost too sick to answer him. Virtue, I was beginning to discover, is by no means its own reward.

A month after, in Humboldt's Bay, that region "at the back of all God-speed", I was talking, in the Chinese store, with a travelling Dutch doctor, a man of considerable scientific attainments. I don't know what induced me to tell him my story, I never expected he would believe it. I do not think he did, but he was extremely polite about it.

"Your description," he said, "suggests a form of life from which all animal life is supposed to have sprung; the amoeba, the blind, formless, embracing mass that eventually differentiated into a thousand higher beings. Minute in size, it still persists, in certain waters. Its discovery of the size you mention would be an epoch."

"It would have made me, wouldn't it?"

His cold eye sparkled. "It would have made and unmade a score of men and a hundred theories. But . . " He was too polite to finish. He changed the subject. "And the remarkable girl," he asked, "what became of her?"

"Oh," I said, staring out to the limitless sea, so seldom ruffled by the keel of any ship, "I was up against it in various ways, and sick of things, so I thought I might as well commit suicide as not."

"Commit—suicide?"

"There are various ways of doing it. I took a way that's not unpleasant . . . I married her."

The Chinaman, as I went out, leaned over his counter to touch my arm. His wrinkled, ancient face was alight with strange feelings.

"Dutchman not light, all long," he whispered. "Me savvy."

I shall never leave the Bay. I have called the girl Amber; she is a good wife. Sometimes I have wondered if she was worth it all. Science is a sacred thing . . . The old Chinaman knows.

The First Wife

Katharine Tynan

The dead woman had lain six years in her grave, and the new wife had reigned five of them in her stead. Her triumph over her dead rival was well-nigh complete. She had nearly ousted her memory from her husband's heart. She had given him an heir for his name and estate, and, lest the bonny boy should fail, there was a little brother creeping on the nursery floor, and another child stirring beneath her heart. The twisted yew before the door, which was heavily buttressed because the legend ran that when it died the family should die out with it, had taken another lease of life, and sent out one spring green shoots on boughs long barren. The old servants had well-nigh forgotten the pale mistress who reigned one short year; and in the fishing village the lavish benefactions of the reigning lady had quite extinguished the memory of the tender voice and gentle words of the woman whose place she filled. A new era of prosperity had come to the Island and the race that long had ruled it.

Under a high, stately window of the ruined Abbey was the dead wife's grave. In the year of his bereavement, before the beautiful brilliant cousin of his dead Alison came and seized on his life, the widower had spent days and nights of stony despair standing by her grave. She had died to give him an heir to his name, and her sacrifice had been vain, for the boy came into the world dead, and lay on her breast in the coffin. Now for years he had not visited the place: the last wreaths of his mourning for her had been washed into earth and dust long ago, and the grave was neglected. The fisherwives whispered that a despairing widower is soonest comforted; and in that haunted Island of ghosts and omens there were those who said that they had met the dead woman gliding at night along the quay under the Abbey walls, with the shape of a child gathered within her shadowy arms. People avoided the quay at night therefore, and no tale of the ghost ever came to the ears of Alison's husband.

His new wife held him indeed in close keeping. In the first days of his re-marriage the servants in the house had whispered that there had been ill blood over the man between the two women, so strenuously did the second wife labour to uproot any trace of the first. The cradle that had been prepared for the young heir was flung to a fishergirl expecting her base-born baby: the small garments into which Alison had sewn her tears with the stitches went the same road. There was many an honest wife might have had the things, but that would not have pleased the grim humour of the second wife towards the woman she had supplanted.

Everything that had been Alison's was destroyed or hidden away. Her rooms were changed out of all memory of her. There was nothing, nothing in the house to recall to her widower her gentleness, or her face as he had last seen it, snow-pale and pure between the long ashen-fair strands of her hair. He never came upon anything that could give him a tender stab with the thought of her. So she was forgotten, and the man was happy with his children and his beautiful passionate wife, and the constant tenderness with which she surrounded every hour of his life.

Little by little she had won over all who had cause to love the dead woman, all human creatures, that is to say: a dog was more faithful and had resisted her. Alison's dog was a terrier, old, shaggy and blear-eyed: he had been young with his dead mistress, and had seemed to grow old when she died. He had fretted incessantly during that year of her husband's widow-hood, whimpering and moaning about the house like a distraught creature, and following the man in a heavy melancholy when he made his pilgrimages to the grave. He continued those pilgrimages after the man had forgotten, but the heavy iron gate of the Abbey clanged in his face, and since he could not reach the grave his visits grew fewer and fewer. But he had not forgotten.

The new mistress had put out all her fascinations to win the dog too, for it seemed that while any living creature clung to the dead woman's memory her triumph was not complete. But the dog, amenable to every one else, was savage to her. All her soft overtures were received with snarling, and an uncovering of the strong white teeth that was dangerous. The woman was not without a heart, except for the dead, and the misery of the dog moved her—his restlessness, his whining, the channels that tears had worn under his faithful eyes. She would have liked to take him up in her arms and comfort him; but once when her pity moved her to attempt it, the dog ran at her ravening. The husband cried out: "Has he hurt you, my Love?" and was for stringing him up. But some compunction stirred in her, and she saved him from the rope, though she made no more attempts to conciliate him.

After that the dog disappeared from the warm living-rooms, where he had been used to stretch on the rug before the leaping wood-fires. It was a cold and stormy autumn, with many shipwrecks, and mourning in the village for drowned husbands and sons, whose little fishing boats had been sucked into the boiling surges. The roar of the wind and the roar of the waves made a perpetual tumult in the air, and the creaking and lashing of the forest trees aided the wild confusion. There were nights when the crested battalions of the waves stormed the hillsides and foamed over the Abbey graves, and weltered about the hearthstones of the high-perched fishing village. When there was not storm there was bitter black frost.

The old house had attics in the gables, seldom visited. You went up from the inhabited portions by a corkscrew staircase, steep as a ladder. The servants did not like the attics. There were creaking footsteps on the floors at night, and sometimes the slamming of a door or the stealthy opening of a window. They complained that locked doors up there flew open, and bolted windows were found un-bolted. In storm the wind keened like a banshee, and one bright snowy morning a housemaid, who had business there, found a slender wet footprint on the floor as of some one who had come barefoot through the snow; and fled down shrieking.

In one of the attics stood a great hasped chest, wherein the dead woman's dresses were mouldering. The chest was locked, and was likely to remain so for long, for the new mistress had flung away the key. From the high attic windows there was a glorious view of sea and land, of the red sandstone valleys where the deer were feeding, of the black tossing woods, of the roan bulls grazing quietly in the park, and far beyond, of the sea, and the fishing fleet, and in the distance the smoke of a passing steamer. But none observed that view. There was not a servant in the house who would lean from the casement without expecting the touch of a clay-cold finger on her shoulder. Any whose business brought them to the attic looked in the corners warily, while they stayed, but the servants did not like to go there alone. They said the room smelt strangely of earth, and that the air struck with an insidious chill: and a gamekeeper being in full view of the attic window one night declared that from the window came a faint moving glow, and that a wavering shadow moved in the room.

It was in this cold attic the dog took up his abode. He followed a servant up there one morning, and broke out into an excited whimpering when he came near the chest. After a while of sniffing and rubbing against it he established himself upon it with his nose on his paws. Afterwards he refused to leave it. Finally the servants gave up the attempt to coax him back into the world, and with a compunctious pity they spread an old rug for him on the chest, and fed him faithfully every day. The master never inquired for him: he was glad to have the brute out of his sight: the mistress heard of the fancy which possessed him, and said nothing: she had given up thinking to win him over. So he grew quite old and grizzled, and half blind as summers and winters passed by. It grew a superstition with the servants to take care of him, and with them on their daily visits he was so affectionate and caressing as to recall the days in which some of them remembered him when his mistress lived, and he was a happy dog, as good at fighting and rat-hunting and weasel-catching as any dog in the Island.

But every night as twelve o'clock struck the dog came down the attic stairs. He was suddenly alert and cheerful, and trotted by an invisible gown. Some said you could hear the faint rustle of silk lapping from stair to stair, and the dog would sometimes bark sharply as in his days of puppyhood, and leap up to lick a hand of air. The servants would shut their doors as they heard the patter of the dog's feet coming, and his sudden bark. They were thrilled with a superstitious awe, but they were not afraid the ghost would harm them. They remembered how just, how gentle, how pure the dead woman had been. They whispered that she might well be dreeing this purgatory of returning to her dispossessed house for another's sake, not her own. Husband and wife were nearly always in their own room when she passed. She went everywhere looking to the fastenings of the house, trying every door and window as she had done in the old days, when her husband declared the old place was only precious because it held her. Presently the servants came to look on her guardianship of the house as holy, for one night some careless person had left a light burning where the wind blew the curtains about, and they took fire, and were extinguished, by whom none knew; but in the morning there was the charred curtain, and Molly, the kitchenmaid, confessed with tears how she had forgotten the lighted candle.

The husband was the last of all to hear of these strange doings, for the new wife took care that they should never be about the house at midnight. But one night as he lay in bed he had forgotten something and asked her to fetch it from below. She looked at him with a disdain out of the mists of her black hair, which she was combing to her knee. Perhaps for a minute she resented his unfaithfulness to the dead. "No," she said, with deliberation, "not till that dog and his companion pass." She flung the door open, and looked half with fear, half with defiance, at the black void outside. There was the patter of the dog's feet coming down the stairs swiftly. The man lifted himself on his elbow and listened. Side by side with the dog's feet came the swish, swish of a silken gown on the stairs. He looked a wild-eyed inquiry at his second wife. She slammed the door to before she answered him. "It has been so for years," she said; "every one knew but you. She has not forgotten as easily as you have."

⁂

One day the dog died, worn out with age. After that they heard the ghost no longer. Perhaps her purgatory of seeing the second wife in her place was completed, and she was fit for Paradise, or her suffering had sufficed to win another's pardon. From that time the new wife reigned without a rival, living or dead, near her throne.

Transmigration

Dora Sigerson Shorter

I.

Many men have tasted Hell some moments of their lives—a Hell of their own making, perhaps; but I, oh God! I have been in the Hell of the damned.

I cannot remember my father or my mother; oh, wretched that I am! Had I either to love one whom no man loves? No, I cannot remember. My memory goes back three months—no further. Every day I live those three months over and over again.

I had too much money when I came of age. I knew not how to use it. I threw it here and there, ever indulging in my own pleasure. Playing in the world till the dust of it rose up and clouded my eyes—till the hand of innocence I held in mine was changed for the hand of sin.

Playing in a world that I was sent to work in, I forgot I had a soul or that there was a God who had given it to me. I played until my selfish indulgences brought upon me the sickness of death. And then my three months of Hell commenced. Unloved, unfriended, I tossed upon my bed, blaspheming a God I did not believe in, swearing I would not die. Shrieking in my terror of that Hell, I felt myself approaching a Hell I had so often scoffed at. I heard my screams re-echo through the empty house, unreplied to, making my desolation complete. Then I lay still, gasping on my bed; so would my prayers soar up to Heaven, I thought, unanswered, unheard. But stay! a step on the stairs—nearer, nearer; the door has opened, and a man stands upon the threshold. Oh, eyes that beamed peace and love, you saved me from Heaven's vengeance for the moment—at what a cost! He came forward into the room when he saw me, and I thought for an instant it was an angel sent to comfort my misery.

"I heard you call," he said; "and, fearing you were ill, I entered. I am your neighbour, my latch-key fits your door. You must pardon my coming, but, thinking you were ill—and alone—"

"I am alone," I said—"alone, alone, deserted alike by God and man. Body and soul I am alone, and sick unto death."

"Despair not, my friend," said he. "I will attend you; you are sick, and morbid from being left alone. Rouse yourself, and I will try and help."

"Help me! no man can help me; I have helped no man. Unless you can give me another life to live with the knowledge I have of this."

"My dear friend, God alone can do that," his voice went on soothingly; "but you are truly sorry for your past?"

"Man," I cried, "there are no such things as death-bed repentances. Death is ever beside us a yawning precipice; as we walk along its edge we *know* that it is there. We look at the sky above it, at the flowers by its brink, but we never look at it; we turn our heads away, but we know that it is there. We feel the chill of it in the heat of the sun. We see its shadow on the petals of the flowers. We know that a false step, a stumble, and we are gone, plunged into Eternity in a moment. We say that some-time this path must come to an end, as we but follow it to our extermination, and when we see before us the black doors of death, *then* will we lay aside our flowers, and still our songs and laughter. And

Heaven will pity our prayers and sighs. Talk not to me of such repentances; I believe them not, nor you, nor any man."

"You are very ill," the stranger said, as I raved on.

"I will not die, I must live, though Heaven itself has shut its gates upon me. Hell—if such is my destination—must give me a year of life. I say, I will not die." A strange strength seemed to flow through my veins. I raised myself on my elbow. The stranger was standing at my bedside looking with divine pity at my convulsed face.

"You," I said. Oh, the horror of it! "You must die, you with your life of purity behind you; death should have no fears for you. The gates of Heaven are open for you; give me your body, your life, and let me live."

"Friend," he said, as though humouring me, "I cannot die; I have a mother who is old and requires my care, and a child, a darling little child."

"You must die!" I cried again. "I will care for your mother and child. You must die and let me live—I say, I will not die."

"You are very ill," was all he said, laying his hand upon my brow. And then, I know not how it came to pass, whether my cry to Heaven or Hell had been answered, or, whatever it was, by some great effort of my will, *but I stood by the bed looking down at my own sleeping body*. I dashed across the room to the glass. It was the stranger it reflected back—yes, the same high forehead, with fair, wavy hair, the same large, dreamy eyes; but his soul, ah! his soul lay sleeping in that motionless form upon the bed. I turned and left the haunted room, living, living, living!

II.

Living, living—oh, the joy of it! I had died and was born again. How it came about, what cared I? "Who," I thought, as I bounded down the stairs, "so fortunate as I?" What man or woman thinking over the past has not said—"Oh, could I but live my life over again, I would not have done this thing or that?" And I, with my evil past laid out before me, could live it again, casting out the weeds and cultivating the trodden flowers; with nothing to hinder me, not even the sensual flesh that lay upstairs, a prison-house for the spirit of that good man whose body I was inhabiting and whose life I proposed to live.

I closed the door of my own house and went up the tiny garden to the next; as I did so, I heard the patter of little feet and a childish voice calling, "Here's papa! Here's papa!"

I opened the door and took the little darling into my arms. Never had I felt such happiness as when the innocent parted lips met mine and the soft baby-hands went round my neck. I stood still to take in the joy of it, but the child drew back in my arms and for a moment she sat quite quiet, and then she struggled until I had to let her down.

"It's not my papa!" she sobbed, running into the little sitting-room. "Oh, gran'ma, 'tis not my own papa!"

Mechanically I hung my hat upon the rack in the hall and followed the child. The room was small, but very bright and cosy; an old lady was seated in an arm-chair before the blazing fire; one withered hand was laid caressingly upon the golden head of the little girl, the other shaded her eyes as she anxiously watched the door. When I entered she smiled and turned to the weeping child.

"Why, what ailed you, darling? Look, Rosy, it is your own papa."

Rosy looked up through her tears, and, seeing me standing in the full glare of the lamp and fire, ran to me again. I sat down in a low chair opposite the old woman, and the little child climbed on to my knees.

"It's my good papa," she said, laying her wet cheek against mine.

For an hour I sat thus tasting for the first time the joy of a home, and listening to the old woman as she told me tales of her son's youth—my youth now.

For some time she rambled on, in the fashion of the old, and at last for very joy I laughed aloud, waking the child, who had fallen asleep in my arms.

"Will you take her up to bed, Gilbert," said her grandmother; "she sat up for you that you might put her to sleep to-night."

I raised the child in my arms, the pretty little babe with her soft curls falling across her face, and she laid her drowsy head upon my shoulder. I pressed her with joy to my breast as I turned up the narrow, dark stairs; at my movement she sat up suddenly and pushed me from her with both her tiny hands. Oh, wonderful instinct of the child that in the light beheld her father, but in darkness knew me for a stranger!

"You're not my papa! Oh, I want papa!"

"Hush, hush!" I whispered; "I am your papa."

"You're not, you're not!" and she beat upon my breast with both her tiny fists.

"Give me my own papa, you bad, bad man!"

Then a great fury seized me, and I held her over the banisters.

"Call me your father, or I let you go."

"No, no; I want my own papa!"

"Call me your father, or I let you go."

"I want my good papa!"

I did not mean it, Heaven knows I did not mean it, but my fingers loosed their hold. I shook the little hands from their terrified grasp upon my coat. The hall echoed the screams of a child and a sickening thud on the flags beneath. A terrible laugh followed, a laugh that might have come from the lowest pits of Hell. Was it I who uttered it?

I looked into the hall beneath me. A trembling old woman knelt there, and, at her side, a servant with a lighted candle, but their white faces were not turned to the motionless body at their feet, but towards me, unspeaking, as though they were frozen by some terrible sight or sound. Had a devil entered into the body of Gilbert Graham during the time my spirit was passing from my own to it—a devil who, making me work its will, thus laughed in its hideous triumph. Surely devils were many round my bed when I lay dying. Its power had left me now, and I went, in bitter remorse, to the little child.

"She slipped from my arms," I whispered. "She slipped, mother."

She answered me nothing; but, as I raised the senseless babe, the servant sobbed, "Oh, Master Gilbert, we thought the shock had sent you mad!"

I laid the child upon the sofa, while the girl ran for a doctor. I stood as though stunned until he came, watching him then in a dream as he examined the soft limbs of the poor babe, and he shook his head as he arose.

"I am sorry to have to tell you that if she lives she will be a cripple all her life."

"Tell my mother," I whispered. I was not the one to tell her this.

"I am sorry," he said; "I am very sorry, Madam."

"Hush!" the old woman answered; "hush! You will waken her."

"She may never waken," he whispered. "Bear up, dear Madam."

"Hush!" the old woman said again, touching the golden curls that were stained with blood. "Hush! The fairies have come to her and laid red poppies in her hair."

And thus had I fulfilled my trust to care for his mother and child—one a cripple or dead, the other a muttering idiot.

I had launched my new life, and the waters that bore it were red human blood; but who or what was the dread pilot that guided it?

III.

I stole out into the dimly lighted street. Of what use was I at home?

The little child still lingered. The old woman was still happy in her ignorance, babbling of fairies and red poppies. My hands were the fairies that had laid those terrible flowers on her babe's fair head, the sleep-giving poppies on her eyes.

The paper-boys were shouting in my ears as I passed, but I paid no attention to them. Their "terrible tragedies" could not equal mine; their cries of "Murder!" woke no horror in my heart; they only cried aloud the word that echoed there. I dare not think of the imprisoned soul that lay as dead in my room—the only one who sought me out in my hour of death's despair. My horrible cries, that had frightened the very servants from my house, but hastened his feet to my side; and now he slept, a thin wall between him and the reward I had given him—a ruined home.

Oh, how could I hear the city noises and a thousand cries within my breast—a thousand little hands beating upon my heart, "Give back! give back!"

And so I strode through the damp fog, caring not, thinking not where I was going. At last a bright light flashed in my eyes, and I started as though awaking. Before me was a lighted doorway, and above it, in the light of the lamp, hung a board, and upon it in red letters the word "Billiards". The place was a gambling-hell. I had known it but too well in the old days. I gazed about, half-hearing some one speaking, and saw a young man before me, his face flushed and his eyelids drooping.

"I could not help it, Graham; indeed I could not! I tried to keep away because of my promise to you and for my mother's sake."

His promise to me! I almost laughed aloud. Yes, I knew that boyish, effeminate face. It had been often opposite to me at the gambling-table inside. I had seen it grow white and tortured as the game went on. I had made its hairless lips grow sweet in a smile, or quiver pathetically like a girl's, by the turn of my hand; I had lured him on night after night with a hope I held between my fingers. His promise to me! I had forgotten. Something evil was rising in my heart. I felt it would claim my lips if I did not speak. I seized his arm.

"Go home," I said; "heed not what I may say to you after this, heed not what I may seem to you. The most beautiful statue is but hollow and moulded in common clay. The tiger's claws are soft as a lady's cheek, but they will tear you to pieces if you trust them. The moth sees the candle's flame, and, thinking it fair, he dies. I am not as you think—"

"I do not know what you mean, Graham. If you mean this den has any fairness for me, it is not so, unless it be the fascination of the bird to the serpent's eye."

"Leave me!" I cried despairingly, for devils' words were rising to my lips; and as he did not heed me, I turned and spoke them.

"Come in with me," I said, and laughed. "Come in with me, and I shall see fair play."

"With you!" He started. "With you, Graham! you who have preached of its dangers to me and its temptations and wickedness; you to whom I looked to save me from where it will lead me. Oh, Graham! I could laugh, 'tis so absurd!"

"I'll see fair play," I said again; "besides, you could not break yourself of the habit so easily and abruptly—I will wean you from it by degrees."

I took his arm, and we passed inside. No one took any notice of me when we entered, but they all gathered around my companion.

"Why, Varen, we thought you were going to leave us?"

"Did you hear of the discovery in Harrington Street last night? Poor Bulger! You remember Bulger, don't you? You lost a cool hundred to him one night here over the cards, eh? Got a cataleptic fit, they say; most interesting case. Went home in a most distressing state of mind the other night, commenced shouting like the devil, frightened the servant out of her wits and out of the house—says she hid in a doorway till dawn, afraid to go back; then she screwed up her courage and stole to the house; finding no answer to her knocks, and being unable to open the door, became alarmed, started for the police-station, and returned with some of the force. One got into the house by a low window and opened the door to the rest; they found poor Bulger lying on his bed—they thought—dead as a herring, but the doctors say 'tis a most interesting case of catalepsy."

I listened without speaking. "What a queer old world it is!" I thought; "we must have a name for everything, no matter how wonderful, or where would our doctors and men of science be? Nothing is left to the God who designed the whole. Our beliefs are superstitions, we laugh them away; we would explain the very law of life itself."

A hand was laid upon my arm.

"Play a game of cards, Graham? The fellows are asking me."

"No, no; this is no place for you—for me. Come out of it quickly."

But the men surrounded us.

"You are not going yet? just one game, then?"

Fool that I was, I complied, and took my seat at the table. They thought I was a "green one", as was evident from their surprised looks when I swept up their little pile of silver at the end of the first game.

"You would think it was old Bulger himself," I heard one say; "he seems to have his accursed luck."

One game led to another; my companion's face grew pale; some demon arose within me, and I took a pleasure in its paleness.

Why is it innocence attracts the guilty so? Behind the bar connected with this card-room there was a young girl serving. I heard men make rude jests that brought the colour to her cheeks; she would hang her head if they called her endearing names, and the angry tears would spring to her eyes: she would shake off their hands with passion. For this girl they would leave their billiards and their cards to watch the red and white fly to her face; and now, when they speak to her, she answers their jests with similar ones; she answers their calls with a simper; she courts their caresses and their company; she is no longer attractive to them—she is one of themselves.

Why did I not pick out my prey among those evil, coarse faces—why did I seek to destroy the one exception? I know not; life preys upon that which is weaker than itself, not that which is its equal.

I swept pile after pile of silver into my pockets, Varen's white face growing whiter and whiter. At last he started to his feet—

"I'm cleared out—I have only a shilling left; I'm going home."

"Put it down," I said to him. "Why, man, you may win a pile on it yet. Finish this round, anyway."

Sullenly he sat down again and took up his cards.

I let him win game after game, and when he rose to depart he had won back a third of his losses.

"I'll come again to-morrow night and win the rest," he said, with a smile.

Why follow the downfall of that young life? Night after night we met in the same place, I hastening away from the ceaseless crying of a little, suffering child, calling for the father I had robbed her of; he from the complaints of a broken-hearted mother, powerless to draw her only son from the snare I had set for him. Night after night I robbed him of his earnings, leaving him to win back a third, to lure him with a hope, never to be fulfilled, that the next time he might win a fortune.

Paler each night grew the young face, shabbier the clothes, thinner the hands that grasped the cards so eagerly. Now he spoke no word of greeting to me; only his eyes revealed his thoughts: therein I could see the light of hope gleam faintly each night, fading, fading to give place to despair, returning again as the closing hours approached and the waiter's voice warned us it was time to stop.

One night Varen came hastily in, staggering as though he were drunk. Flinging himself down in a chair, he took his cards. There was no hope in his eyes; I saw only terrible anguish and despair. On one sleeve of his shabby coat I saw a broad band of crape.

He played wildly—and won. I had slain my devil; he won again; I was glad. I saw his silver flow back to him; I was happy for the first time in many a weary hour. "I shall no longer be his curse," I thought; "through me he shall win back his fortune, his mother's blessing, his lost youth. I shall restore all."

A cry recalled me. I had been dreaming. I gazed around bewildered; the candles were spluttering in their sockets, and on the side of one was a great roll of wax. It was turned towards Varen—I had heard old wives call it a winding-sheet. The dust of the day before lay white on the sideboard and table, disturbed only where the cards fell and by the track of our fingers. The dawn was creeping through the half-closed shutters of the window, making our faces grey and ghastly in the two lights.

Young Varen was staring at me with mad eyes, and on the table at my side lay a heap of silver. It was I who had been winning.

Varen leaned across the table and gazed into my face.

"Are you a man," he said, "or are you a devil?"

I did not answer, but that terrible thing within me broke into a laugh. The men beside me started in horror as the sound came forth and echoed round the room as though a demon were in each corner to repeat it

Varen's hand went to his breast.

"Devil in the shape of a man," he said, "your work is done. Cruellest of enemies in the guise of a friend! You won my trust and led me to this. What is pure, since you I believed so pure are as you are? What is the reward of love, since you I have loved reward me so? Through your aid I was fighting the old life from me, and rising to honour and esteem, to the knowledge of a mother's proud heart. And through your aid I fell to meanness and disgrace, to see a mother robbed of her necessaries, and worse—to lose her son's love and care and to die broken-hearted alone. Your hand had saved me from the precipice of Hell, and your hand it is that flings me into its hottest fire. Finish, then, your devil's work, for I dare not!"

He drew a pistol from his breast and handed it to me. I felt the cold steel in my hand, and saw the horrified looks of the men around us; they seemed powerless to cry out or interrupt us; before me the ghastly face of young Varen. A wild rage rose up in my heart; I panted like a mad dog, and foam fell from my mouth. I tried to pray, but could not.

A pistol-shot rang through the room, and the white face before me vanished. There was hot blood upon my hands; a terror seized me—what had I done? Hands were upon my shoulders. But I escaped them. I flew down the creaking stairs. People were shouting. Steps were coming after me. I flung wide the door and flew wildly, blindly, down the street. Feet were repeating the echo of mine. People were calling "Murder! murder!" Windows were flung open, men joined in the chase. People were calling "Murder!"—and my hands were red with blood. Ha! the well-known door—it was my own; *his* latch-key opened it. I let myself in and flew upstairs; there was a light in my old room; a nurse sat nodding over the fire. I saw my old form lying motionless upon the bed. I sprang to its side. Voices were calling at the hall-door—men were breaking it in. They had tracked me.

I seized the hand that lay upon the counter-pane; a shudder ran through it. Steps were at the door, "Murder" ran through the house. There was a moment of nothingness and I woke.

It was all a terrible dream; I lay upon my own bed. The kind neighbour, hearing my cry, had called in to see if I needed anything; he was looking down with pity in his eyes, his hands cooling mine—he had dipped them in water. No! it was blood, BLOOD! and the room rang with the cries of "MURDERER!" I started up; they were putting manacles on his wrists. He was stunned, he knew not what to say; he answered not their insinuations, but passed his manacled hands now and again across his eyes, like a man who had been long sleeping.

A terrible laugh sounded round the room; it seemed to float through the doorway, and we heard it echo down the house, fading away into stillness. I tried to rise and speak, but fell back unconscious.

IV.

I awoke to misery and despair. Lying still a moment, to gather my thoughts together, I heard some persons talking at the head of my bed. It was the nurse and a couple of men, doctors I soon knew them to be. They were talking excitedly, but in subdued voices; I heard every word distinctly: "Graham is to be hanged for the murder of young Varen." I started up, gazing at them in agony.

"He did not do it. I, and I alone, am guilty."

They had started back when I moved, in astonishment; but when I spoke they came beside me, trying to soothe me and make me lie down and rest again. To rest! O Heaven! there was no more rest for me in this world.

I told them I would explain, but they would not let me speak. I heard them whisper of my most extraordinary case. They thought I had gained consciousness while they were speaking of Graham, and, hearing their words at that critical moment, took the idea into my head that I had committed the crime.

"Let me go!" I moaned; "let me go!"

But they held me down in their cruel kindness till I had to do their bidding from very weakness.

But when the night came on, and when the old nurse was nodding in her chair, I arose in the darkness and went from the house. Up and down the streets I wandered till dawn grew gray, but no dawn arose in my heart, only black night for ever. Through the streets, never stopping, I walked till the sun grew hot and bright, and people crowded out into the pathways. I bought a paper from a newsvendor, and read the trial of Gilbert Graham. It was nearly over; all the evidence was against him. He had nothing to say for himself; once he spoke to ask if he might see his little child, and he was told she was dead. They said he seemed stunned, or as though in a dream. I read no more.

When the court was opened, and the trial came on again, I hid myself among the crowd that attended it. I saw the prisoner at the bar; he was not pale; a colour tinged his cheeks. He seemed as if he were asleep. I do not think he heard anything of what was going on. Witness after witness came to condemn him. I could not bear it. I put myself forward as a witness for the defence. They allowed me into the box. I tried to tell my story, but they would not listen to me; some laughed; some pitied me; but they would not let me speak.

"Will you not hear me?" I cried. "You cannot understand, but do not laugh; there are so many things men know nothing of, but do not scorn them because you do not understand them. Can you know what gives life to the smallest insect living on this earth? Can you explore a step beyond the grave? You cannot. I alone am guilty of this murder; by my own act, or by the act of Heaven or Hell, I know not."

A gentleman rose in the court; he sent a message to the Judge, whispered to a constable, and I was dragged out of the house. I heard a murmur of excited voices and a whisper.

" 'Tis that poor fellow Bulger; they say his brain is turned since he had his cataleptic attack."

I was forced along by my doctor, his arm linked in mine. Calling a cab, he put me inside, and was about to follow, when a friend of his came up and spoke to him.

"Oh, yes," he answered, "I thought I'd find him there. He woke to consciousness just as Dr. Gill and myself were speaking of young Varen's death, and he seemed to get it into his head that he was the murderer. He escaped from the house last night, but from his ravings I thought it probable I should find him at court to-day."

I heard no more. Silently opening the door furthest from the speaker, I slipped out, and in the dusk of the evening made my escape.

How the night passed I know not, but, when the light came, I had but one thought: to seek out Graham and beg his forgiveness. Again I bought a morning paper, and read the finish of the trial. Graham was condemned to death.

After a day's wandering, or maybe more—I knew nothing of time in those blank hours—I found out the prison where he lay awaiting his doom, and craved admittance, saying I was a particular friend—a friend!

They let me see him for a moment, but he did not know me. He even smiled when I asked his forgiveness; even he would not believe me.

"I do not understand it at all," he said, laying his head on his hand wearily. "I cannot think, I cannot even feel these last few days," and then raised his head and gazed at me eagerly. "Do you know anything of my mother?"

I did not know of her, and turned away my face.

"I had a child!" he cried. "Oh, tell me of my little child!"

"Do you not remember?—she is dead," I told him, weeping.

He leaned his head upon his hand again. "I had forgotten."

He spoke no more to me, and I was taken out of the place. "He will forgive me to-morrow," I said.

But, hidden away in a low lodging-house, I was too ill to stir for many days; then early one morning I found myself at the prison door again; it opened for me readily, and when it closed I found myself confronted by my doctor and some of his friends.

"I thought our patient would turn up sooner or later," he said. "How fortunate you should choose the time we are here!"

"I will go anywhere you will if you but let me see him once again," I cried; "only once till he forgives me. Let me go! I must!" I cried, fighting them. "I cannot live unless I get his pardon."

"You cannot see him," they said.

"But I will—I must!"

"You cannot—he was hanged this morning at seven."

Not to Be Taken at Bed-Time

Rosa Mulholland

This is the legend of a house called the Devil's Inn, standing in the heather on the top of the Connemara mountains, in a shallow valley hollowed between five peaks. Tourists sometimes come in sight of it on September evenings; a crazy and weather-stained apparition, with the sun glaring at it angrily between the hills, and striking its shattered window-panes. Guides are known to shun it, however.

The house was built by a stranger, who came no one knew whence, and whom the people nicknamed Coll Dhu (Black Coll), because of his sullen bearing and solitary habits. His dwelling they called the Devil's Inn, because no tired traveller had ever been asked to rest under its roof, nor friend known to cross its threshold. No one bore him company in his retreat but a wizen-faced old man, who shunned the good-morrow of the trudging peasant when he made occasional excursions to the nearest village for provisions for himself and master, and who was as secret as a stone concerning all the antecedents of both.

For the first year of their residence in the country, there had been much speculation as to who they were, and what they did with themselves up there among the clouds and eagles. Some said that Coll Dhu was a scion of the old family from whose hands the surrounding lands had passed;

and that, embittered by poverty and pride, he had come to bury himself in solitude, and brood over his misfortunes. Others hinted of crime, and flight from another country; others again whispered of those who were cursed from their birth, and could never smile, nor yet make friends with a fellow-creature till the day of their death. But when two years had passed, the wonder had somewhat died out, and Coll Dhu was little thought of, except when a shepherd looking for sheep crossed the track of a big dark man walking the mountains gun in hand, to whom he did not dare say "Lord save you!" or when a housewife rocking the cradle of a winter's night, crossed herself as a gust of a storm thundered over her cabin-roof, with the exclamation, "Oh, then, it's Coll Dhu that has enough o' the fresh air about his head up there this night, the creature!"

Coll Dhu had lived thus in his solitude for some years, when it became known that Colonel Blake, the new lord of the soil, was coming to visit the country. By climbing one of the peaks encircling his eyrie, Coll could look sheer down a mountain-side, and see in miniature beneath him, a grey old dwelling with ivied chimneys and weather-slated walls, standing amongst straggling trees and grim warlike rocks, that gave it the look of a fortress, gazing out to the Atlantic for ever with the eager eyes of all its windows, as if demanding perpetually, "What tidings from the New World?"

He could see now masons and carpenters crawling about below, like ants in the sun, over-running the old house from base to chimney, daubing here and knocking there, tumbling down walls that looked to Coll, up among the clouds, like a handful of jack-stones, and building up others that looked like the toy fences in a child's farm. Through-out several months he must have watched the busy ants at their task of breaking and mending again, disfiguring and beautifying; but when all was done he had not the curiosity to stride down and admire the handsome panelling of the new billiard-room, nor yet the fine view which the enlarged bay-window in the drawing-room commanded of the watery highway to Newfoundland.

Deep summer was melting into autumn, and the amber streaks of decay were beginning to creep out and trail over the ripe purple of moor and mountain, when Colonel Blake, his only daughter, and a party of friends, arrived in the country. The grey house below was alive with gaiety, but Coll Dhu no longer found an interest in observing from his eyrie. When he watched the sun rise or set, he chose to ascend some crag that looked on no human habitation. When he sallied forth on his excursions, gun in hand, he set his face towards the most isolated wastes, dipping into the loneliest valleys, and scaling the nakedest ridges. When he came by chance within call of other excursionists, gun in hand he plunged into the shade of some hollow, and avoided an encounter. Yet it was fated, for all that, that he and Colonel Blake should meet.

Towards the evening of one bright September day, the wind changed, and in half an hour the mountains were wrapped in a thick blinding mist. Coll Dhu was far from his den, but so well had he searched these mountains, and inured himself to their climate, that neither storm, rain, nor fog, had power to disturb him. But while he stalked on his way, a faint and agonised cry from a human voice reached him through the smothering mist. He quickly tracked the sound, and gained the side of a man who was stumbling along in danger of death at every step.

"Follow me!" said Coll Dhu to this man, and, in an hour's time, brought him safely to the lowlands, and up to the walls of the eager-eyed mansion.

"I am Colonel Blake," said the frank soldier, when, having left the fog behind them, they stood in the starlight under the lighted windows. "Pray tell me quickly to whom I owe my life."

As he spoke, he glanced up at his benefactor, a large man with a sombre sun-burned face.

"Colonel Blake," said Coll Dhu, after a strange pause, "your father suggested to my father to stake his estates at the gaming-table. They were staked, and the tempter won. Both are dead; but you and I live, and I have sworn to injure you."

The colonel laughed good humouredly at the uneasy face above him.

"And you began to keep your oath tonight by saving my life?" said he. "Come! I am a soldier, and know how to meet an enemy; but I had far rather meet a friend. I shall not be happy till you have eaten my salt. We have merrymaking tonight in honour of my daughter's birthday. Come in and join us?"

Coll Dhu looked at the earth doggedly.

"I have told you," he said, "who and what I am, and I will not cross your threshold."

But at this moment (so runs the story) a French window opened among the flower-beds by which they were standing, and a vision appeared which stayed the words on Coll's tongue. A stately girl, clad in white satin, stood framed in the ivied window, with the warm light from within streaming around her richly-moulded figure into the night. Her face was as pale as her gown, her eyes were swimming in tears, but a firm smile sat on her lips as she held out both hands to her father. The light behind her touched the glistening folds of her dress—the lustrous pearls round her throat—the coronet of blood-red roses which encircled the knotted braids at the back of her head. Satin, pearls, and roses—had Coll Dhu, of the Devil's Inn, never set eyes upon such things before?

Evleen Blake was no nervous tearful miss. A few quick words—"Thank God! you're safe; the rest have been home an hour"—and a tight pressure of her father's fingers between her own jewelled hands, were all that betrayed the uneasiness she had suffered.

"Faith, my love, I owe my life to this brave gentleman!" said the blithe colonel. "Press him to come in and be our guest, Evleen. He wants to retreat to his mountains, and lose himself again in the fog where I found him; or, rather, where he found me! Come, sir" (to Coll), "you must surrender to this fair besieger."

An introduction followed. "Coll Dhu!" murmured Evleen Blake, for she had heard the common tales of him; but with a frank welcome she invited her father's preserver to taste the hospitality of that father's house.

"I beg you to come in, sir," she said; "but for you our gaiety must have been turned into mourning. A shadow will be upon our mirth if our benefactor disdains to join in it."

With a sweet grace, mingled with a certain hauteur from which she was never free, she extended her white hand to the tall looming figure outside the window; to have it grasped and wrung in a way that made the proud girl's eyes flash their amazement, and the same little hand clench itself in displeasure, when it had hid itself like an outraged thing among the shining folds of her gown. Was this Coll Dhu mad, or rude?

The guest no longer refused to enter, but followed the white figure into a little study where a lamp burned; and the gloomy stranger, the bluff colonel, and the young mistress of the house, were fully discovered to each other's eyes. Evleen glanced at the newcomer's dark face, and shuddered with a feeling of indescribable dread and dislike; then, to her father, accounted for the shudder after a popular fashion, saying lightly: "There is someone walking over my grave."

So Coll Dhu was present at Evleen Blake's birthday ball. Here he was, under a roof which ought to have been his own, a stranger, known only by a nickname, shunned and solitary. Here he was, who had lived among the eagles and foxes, lying in wait with a fell purpose, to be revenged on the son of his father's foe for poverty and disgrace, for the broken heart of a dead mother, for the loss of a self-slaughtered father, for the dreary scattering of brothers and sisters. Here he stood, a Samson shorn of his strength; and all because a haughty girl had melting eyes, a winning mouth, and looked radiant in satin and roses.

Peerless where many were lovely, she moved among her friends, trying to be unconscious of the gloomy fire of those strange eyes which followed her unweariedly wherever she went. And when her father begged her to be gracious to the unsocial guest whom he would fain conciliate, she courteously conducted him to the new picture-gallery adjoining the drawing-rooms; explained under what odd circumstances the colonel had picked up this little painting or that; using every delicate art her pride would allow to achieve her father's purpose, whilst maintaining at the same time her own personal reserve; trying to divert the guest's oppressive attention from herself to the objects for which she claimed his notice. Coll Dhu followed his conductress and listened to her voice, but what she said mattered nothing; nor did she wring many words of comment or reply from his lips, until they paused in a retired corner where the light was dim, before a window from which the curtain was withdrawn. The sashes were open, and nothing was visible but water; the night Atlantic, with the full moon riding high above a bank of clouds, making silvery tracks outward towards the distance of infinite mystery dividing two worlds. Here the following little scene is said to have been enacted.

"This window of my father's own planning, is it not creditable to his taste?" said the young hostess, as she stood, herself glittering like a dream of beauty, looking on the moonlight.

Coll Dhu made no answer; but suddenly, it is said, asked her for a rose from a cluster of flowers that nestled in the lace on her bosom.

For the second time that night Evleen Blake's eyes flashed with no gentle light. But this man was the saviour of her father. She broke off a blossom, and with such good grace, and also with such queen-like dignity as she might assume, presented it to him. Whereupon, not only was the rose seized, but also the hand that gave it, which was hastily covered with kisses.

Then her anger burst upon him.

"Sir," she cried, "if you are a gentleman you must be mad! If you are not mad, then you are not a gentleman!"

"Be merciful," said Coll Dhu; "I love you. My God, I never loved a woman before! Ah!" he cried, as a look of disgust crept over her face, "you hate me. You shuddered the first time your eyes met mine. I love you, and you hate me!"

"I do," cried Evleen, vehemently, forgetting everything but her indignation. "Your presence is like something evil to me. Love me?—your looks poison me. Pray, sir, talk no more to me in this strain."

"I will trouble you no longer," said Coll Dhu. And, stalking to the window, he placed one powerful hand upon the sash, and vaulted from it out of her sight.

Bare-headed as he was, Coll Dhu strode off to the mountains, but not towards his own home. All the remaining dark hours of that night he is believed to have walked the labyrinths of the hills, until dawn began to scatter the clouds with a high wind. Fasting, and on foot from sunrise the morning before, he was then glad enough to see a cabin right in his way. Walking in, he asked for water to drink, and a corner where he might throw himself to rest.

There was a wake in the house, and the kitchen was full of people, all wearied out with the night's watch; old men were dozing over their pipes in the chimney-corner, and here and there a woman was fast asleep with her head on a neighbour's knee. All who were awake crossed themselves when Coll Dhu's figure darkened the door, because of his evil name; but an old man of the house invited him in, and offering him milk, and promising him a roasted potato by-and-by, conducted him to a small room off the kitchen, one end of which was strewed with heather, and where there were only two women sitting gossiping over a fire.

"A thraveller," said the old man, nodding his head at the women, who nodded back, as if to say "he has the traveller's right." And Coll Dhu flung himself on the heather, in the furthest corner of the narrow room.

The women suspended their talk for a while; but presently, guessing the intruder to be asleep, resumed it in voices above a whisper. There was but a patch of window with the grey dawn behind it, but Coll could see the figures by the firelight over which they bent: an old woman sitting forward with her withered hands extended to the embers, and a girl reclining against the hearth wall, with her healthy face, bright eyes, and crimson draperies, glowing by turns in the flickering blaze.

"I do' know," said the girl, "but it's the quarest marriage iver I h'ard of. Sure, it's not three weeks since he tould right an' left that he hated her like poison!"

"Whist, asthoreen!" said the colliagh, bending forward confidentially; "throth an' we all know that o' him. But what could he do, the crature! When she put the burragh-bos on him!"

"The *what?*" asked the girl.

"Then the burragh-bos machree-o? That's the spanchel o' death, avourneen; an' well she has him tethered to her now, bad luck to her!"

The old woman rocked herself and stifled the Irish cry breaking from her wrinkled lips by burying her face in her cloak.

"But what is it?" asked the girl, eagerly. "What's the burragh-bos, anyways, an' where did she get it?"

"Och, och! it's not fit for comin' over to young ears, but cuggir (whisper), acushla! It's a sthrip o' the skin o' a corpse, peeled from the crown o' the head to the heel, without crack or split, or the charm's broke; an' that, rowled up, and put on a sthring roun' the neck o' the wan that's cowld by the wan that wants to be loved. An' sure enough it puts the fire in their hearts, hot an' sthrong, afore twinty-four hours is gone."

The girl had started from her lazy attitude, and gazed at her companion with eyes dilated by horror.

"Marciful Saviour!" she cried. "Not a sowl on airth would bring the curse out o' heaven by sich a black doin'!"

"Aisy, Biddeen alanna! an' there's wan that does it, an' isn't the devil. Arrah, asthoreen, did ye niver hear tell o' Pexie na Pishrogie, that lives betune two hills o' Maam Turk?"

"I h'ard o' her," said the girl, breathlessly.

"Well, sorra bit lie, but it's hersel' that does it. She'll do it for money any day. Sure they hunted her from the graveyard o' Salruck, where she had the dead raised; an' glory be to God! they would ha' murthered her, only they missed her thracks, an' couldn't bring it home to her afther."

"Whist, a-wauher" (my mother)," said the girl; "here's the thraveller getting up to set off on his road again! Och, then, it's the short rest he tuk, the sowl!"

It was enough for Coll, however. He had got up, and now went back to the kitchen, where the old man had caused a dish of potatoes to be roasted, and earnestly pressed his visitor to sit down and eat of them. This Coll did readily; having recruited his strength by a meal, he betook himself to the mountains again, just as the rising sun was flashing among the waterfalls, and sending the night mists drifting down the glens. By sundown the same evening he was striding over the hills of Maam Turk, asking of shepherds his way to the cabin of one Pexie na Pishrogie.

In a hovel on a brown desolate heath, with scared-looking hills flying off into the distance on every side, he found Pexie: a yellow-faced hag, dressed in a dark-red blanket, with elf-locks of coarse black hair protruding from under an orange kerchief swathed round her wrinkled jaws. She was bending over a pot upon her fire, where herbs were simmering, and she looked up with an evil glance when Coll Dhu darkened her door.

"The burragh-bos is it her honour wants?" she asked, when he had made known his errand.

"Ay, ay; but the arrighad, the arrighad (money) for Pexie. The burragh-bos is ill to get."

"I will pay," said Coll Dhu, laying a sovereign on the bench before her.

The witch sprang upon it, and chuckling, bestowed on her visitor a glance which made even Coll Dhu shudder.

"Her honour is a fine king," she said, "an' her is fit to get the burragh-bos. Ha! Ha! her sall get the burragh-bos from Pexie. But the arrighad is not enough. More, more!"

She stretched out her claw-like hand, and Coll dropped another sovereign into it. Whereupon she fell into more horrible convulsions of delight.

"Hark ye!" cried Coll. "I have paid you well, but if your infernal charm does not work, I will have you hunted for a witch!"

"Work!" cried Pexie, rolling up her eyes. "If Pexie's charm not work, then her honour come back here an' carry these bits o' mountain away on her back. Ay, her will work. If the colleen hate her honour like the old diaoul hersel', still an' withal her love will love her honour like her own white sowl afore the sun sets or rises. That (with a furtive leer), or the colleen dhas go wild mad afore wan hour."

"Hag!" returned Coll Dhu; "the last part is a hellish invention of your own. I heard nothing of madness. If you want more money, speak out, but play none of your hideous tricks on me."

The witch fixed her cunning eyes on him, and took her cue at once from his passion.

"Her honour guess thrue," she simpered; "it is only the little bit more arrighad poor Pexie want."

Again the skinny hand was extended. Coll Dhu shrank from touching it, and threw his gold coin upon the table.

"King, king!" chuckled Pexie. "Her honour is a grand king. Her honour is fit to get the burragh-bos. The colleen dhas sall love her like her own white sowl. Ha, ha!"

"When shall I get it?" asked Coll Dhu, impatiently.

"Her honour sall come back to Pexie in so many days, do-deag (twelve), so many days, fur that the burragh-bos is hard to get. The lonely graveyard is far away, an' the dead man is hard to raise—"

"Silence!" cried Coll Dhu; "not a word more. I will have your hideous charm, but what it is, or where you get it, I will not know."

Then, promising to come back in twelve days, he took his departure. Turning to look back when a little way across the heath, he saw Pexie gazing after him, standing on her black hill in relief against the lurid flames of the dawn, seeming to his dark imagination like a fury with all hell at her back.

At the appointed time Coll Dhu got the promised charm. He sewed it with perfumes into a cover of cloth of gold, and slung it to a fine-wrought chain. Lying in a casket which had once held the jewels of Coll's broken-hearted mother, it looked a glittering bauble enough. Meantime the people of the mountains were cursing over their cabin fires, because there had been another unholy raid upon their graveyard, and were banding themselves to hunt the criminal down.

A fortnight passed. How or where could Coll Dhu find an opportunity to put the charm round the neck of the colonel's proud daughter? More gold was dropped into Pexie's greedy claw, and then she promised to assist him in his dilemma.

Next morning the witch dressed herself in decent garb, smoothed her elf-locks under a snowy cap, smoothed the wrinkles out of her face, and with a basket on her arm locked the door of the hovel, and took her way to the lowlands. Pexie seemed to have given up her disreputable calling for that of a simple mushroom-gatherer. The housekeeper at the grey house bought poor Muireade's mushrooms off her every morning. Every morning she left unfailingly a nosegay of wild flowers for Miss Evleen Blake, "God bless her! She had never seen the darling young lady with her own two longing eyes, but sure hadn't she heard tell of her sweet purty face, miles away!" And at last, one morning, whom should she meet but Miss Evleen herself returning alone from a ramble. Whereupon poor Muireade "made bold" to present her flowers in person.

"Ah," said Evleen, "it is you who leave me the flowers every morning? They are very sweet."

Muireade had sought her only for a look at her beautiful face. And now that she had seen it, as bright as the sun, and as fair as the lily, she would take up her basket and go away contented.

Yet she lingered a little longer.

"My lady never walk up big mountain?" said Pexie.

"No," said Evleen, laughing; she feared she could not walk up a mountain.

"Ah yes; my lady ought to go, with more gran' ladies an' gentlemen, ridin' on purty little donkeys, up the big mountains. Oh, gran' things up big mountains for my lady to see!"

Thus she set to work, and kept her listener enchained for an hour, while she related wonderful stories of those upper regions. And as Evleen looked up to the burly crowns of the hills, perhaps she thought there might be sense in this wild old woman's suggestion. It ought to be a grand world up yonder.

Be that as it may, it was not long after this when Coll Dhu got notice that a party from the grey house would explore the mountains next day; that Evleen Blake would be one of the number; and that he, Coll, must prepare to house and refresh a crowd of weary people, who in the evening should be brought, hungry and faint, to his door. The simple mushroom-gatherer should be discovered laying in her humble stock among the green places between the hills, should volunteer to act as guide to the party, should lead them far out of their way through the mountains and up and down the most toilsome ascents and across dangerous places; to escape safely from which, the servants should be told to throw away the baskets of provisions which they carried.

Coll Dhu was not idle. Such a feast was set forth, as had never been spread so near the clouds before. We are told of wonderful dishes furnished by unwholesome agency, and from a place believed much hotter than is necessary for purposes of cookery. We are told also how Coll Dhu's barren chambers were suddenly hung with curtains of velvet, and with fringes of gold; how the blank white walls glowed with delicate colours and gilding; how gems of pictures sprang into sight between the panels; how the tables blazed with plate and gold, and glittered with the rarest glass; how such wines flowed, as the guests had never tasted; how servants in the richest livery, amongst whom the wizen-faced old man was a mere nonentity, appeared, and stood ready to carry in the wonderful dishes, at whose extraordinary fragrance the eagles came pecking to the windows, and the foxes drew near the walls, snuffing. Sure enough, in all good time, the weary party came within sight of the Devil's Inn, and Coll Dhu sallied forth to invite them across his lonely threshold. Colonel Blake (to whom Evleen, in her delicacy, had said no word of the solitary's strange behaviour to herself) hailed his appearance with delight, and the whole party sat down to Coll's banquet in high good humour. Also, it is said, in much amazement at the magnificence of the mountain recluse.

All went in to Coll's feast, save Evleen Blake, who remained standing on the threshold of the outer door; weary, but unwilling to rest there; hungry, but unwilling to eat there. Her white cambric dress was gathered on her arms, crushed and sullied with the toils of the day; her bright cheek was a little sun-burned; her small dark head with its braids a little tossed, was bared to the mountain air and the glory of the sinking sun; her hands were loosely tangled in the strings of her hat; and her foot sometimes tapped the threshold-stone. So she was seen.

The peasants tell that Coll Dhu and her father came praying her to enter, and that the magnificent servants brought viands to the threshold; but no step would she move inward, no morsel would she taste.

"Poison, poison!" she murmured, and threw the food in handfuls to the foxes, who were snuffing on the heath.

But it was different when Muireade, the kindly old woman, the simple mushroom-gatherer, with all the wicked wrinkles smoothed out of her face, came to the side of the hungry girl, and coaxingly presented a savoury mess of her own sweet mushrooms, served on a common earthen platter.

"An' darlin', my lady, poor Muireade her cook them hersel', an' no thing o' this house touch them or look at poor Muireade's mushrooms."

Then Evleen took the platter and ate a delicious meal. Scarcely was it finished when a heavy drowsiness fell upon her, and, unable to sustain herself on her feet, she presently sat down upon the door-stone. Leaning her head against the framework of the door, she was soon in a deep sleep, or trance. So she was found.

"Whimsical, obstinate little girl!" said the colonel, putting his hand on the beautiful slumbering head. And taking her in his arms he carried her into a chamber which had been (say the story-tellers) nothing but a bare and sorry closet in the morning but which was now fitted up with Oriental splendour. And here on a luxurious couch she was laid, with a crimson coverlet wrapping her feet. And here in the tempered light coming through jewelled glass, where yesterday had been a coarse rough-hung window, her father looked his last upon her lovely face.

The colonel returned to his host and friends, and by-and-by the whole party sallied forth to see the after-glare of a fierce sunset swathing the hills in flames. It was not until they had gone some distance that Coll Dhu remembered to go back and fetch his telescope. He was not long absent. But he was absent long enough to enter that glowing chamber with a stealthy step, to throw a light chain around the neck of the sleeping girl, and to slip among the folds of her dress the hideous glittering burragh-bos.

After he had gone away again, Pexie came stealing to the door, and, opening it a little, sat down on the mat outside, with her cloak wrapped round her. An hour passed, and Evleen Blake still slept, her breathing scarcely stirring the deadly bauble on her breast. After that, she began to murmur and moan and Pexie pricked up her ears. Presently a sound in the room told her that the victim was awake and had risen. Then Pexie put her face to the aperture of the door and looked in, gave a howl of dismay, and fled from the house, to be seen in that country no more.

The light was fading among the hills, and the ramblers were returning towards the Devil's Inn, when a group of ladies who were considerably in advance of the rest, met Evleen Blake advancing towards them on the heath, with her hair disordered as by sleep, and no covering on her head. They noticed something bright, like gold, shifting and glancing with the motion of her figure. There had been some jesting among them about Evleen's fancy for falling asleep on the door-step instead of coming in to dinner, and they advanced laughing, to rally her on the subject.

But she stared at them in a strange way, as if she did not know them, and passed on. Her friends were rather offended, and commented on her fantastic humour; only one looked after her, and got laughed at by her companions for expressing uneasiness on the wilful young lady's account.

So they kept their way, and the solitary figure went fluttering on, the white robe blushing, and the fatal burragh-bos glittering in the reflection from the sky. A hare crossed her path, and she laughed out loudly, and clapping her hands, sprang after it. Then she stopped and asked questions of the stones, striking them with her open palm because they would not answer. (An amazed shepherd sitting behind a rock witnessed these strange proceedings.) By-and-by she began to call after the birds, in a wild shrill way startling the echoes of the hills as she went along. A party of gentlemen returning by a dangerous path, heard the unusual sound and stopped to listen.

"What is that?" asked one.

"A young eagle," said Coll Dhu, whose face had become livid, "they often give such cries."

"It was uncommonly like a woman's voice!" was the reply; and immediately another wild note rang towards them from the rocks above; a bare saw-like ridge, shelving away to some distance ahead, and projecting one hungry tooth over an abyss. A few more moments and they saw Evleen Blake's light figure fluttering out towards this dizzy point.

"My Evleen!" cried the colonel, recognising his daughter, "she is mad to venture on such a spot!"

"Mad!" repeated Coll Dhu. And then he dashed off to the rescue with all the might and swiftness of his powerful limbs.

When he drew near her, Evleen had almost reached the verge of the terrible rock. Very cautiously he approached her, his object being to seize her in his strong arms before she was aware of his presence, and carry her many yards away from the spot of danger. But in a fatal moment Evleen turned her head and saw him. One wild ringing cry of hate and horror, which startled the very eagles and scattered a flight of curlews above her head, broke from her lips. A step backward brought her within a foot of death.

One desperate though wary stride, and she was struggling in Coll's embrace. One glance in her eyes, and he saw that he was striving with a mad woman. Back, back, she dragged him, and he had nothing to grasp by. The rock was slippery and his shod feet would not cling to it. Back, back! A hoarse panting, a dire swinging to and fro; and then the rock was standing naked against the sky, no one was there, and Coll Dhu and Evleen Blake lay shattered far below.

The Red Woollen Necktie

B. M. Croker

"I had a dream which was not all a dream." – Byron.

When this century had reached the age allotted to man, and I was but yet in my teens, we lived in a rambling old place in the west, called Coolnafinn. My father, Colonel Mardall, succeeded to this property at a truly propitious moment; for just as he was "kicked out" of the service, for age, another career opened its arms to him—one almost as exciting and uncertain—in short, the career of an Irish landlord.

We found Coolnafinn in surprisingly good repair, surrounded by a fine well-timbered demesne, and, imposing as it was isolated, the house stood at the junction of the back and front avenues, which were each a mile in length. We were four miles from church, ten from our post town, and fifteen from a station; neighbours were few and far between, but we were a host in ourselves—seven motherless boys and girls,— and the roomy old mansion, great walled gardens, orchards and grounds, proved a delightful change from barrack quarters, and the narrow limits of the conventional furnished house of a garrison town.

The experience that I am about to relate occurred when I was nineteen, that is to say, when chignons and croquet were the fashion. In spite of my years I was credited with an old head on young shoulders, and was the mistress of my father's establishment, and keeper of the keys—no easy post, considering that I had to deal with six boisterous and critical young relatives.

I shared the same room with my sister Fanny. It was the best bedroom—a great lofty apartment with three bow windows. One hot July night, I could not sleep for ages—I tumbled and tossed; I got up and drank water; I counted the prescribed "hundred sleep"; I watched the moonlight steal in between the blinds, and touch each separate object on which it fell, with a pale, weird light; I felt cold, shivering, frightened—but why? I did not believe in ghosts. I was not alone, for there was Fanny in an opposite bed, breathing regularly, and evidently far away in the land of dreams. What ailed me? Why was I conscious of a beating heart, accompanied by a scarcely defined, but undeniable dread? At last I "fell off," and I dreamt—though all the time, even in my dream, I said to myself, "This is not a dream; it is real."

It seemed as if the house, for some un-explained reason, was empty; I was absolutely alone, sitting reading in the drawing-room with my back to one of the long French windows which opened to the ground. Suddenly a dark shadow came between me and the light, and, turning round, I beheld a tall, powerful man, with his head pressed closely against the glass; his face was shaded by a weather-beaten wide-awake, or caubeen; he was dressed like a tramp, and the only thing I particularly noticed about him was a pair of very large, dirty hands, and a red worsted necktie.

He remained for some seconds leaning against the sash, and gazing intently into the room; then I started to my feet, and called out—

"What do you want?"

"Is the colonel within?" he asked, in a hoarse voice.

"No, he is out," I screamed in reply.

"I want to see him badly. I served under him wance. Is Master Robin, or Master Ted, in?"

I shook my head.

"I've come a terrible long way"—holding up a large foot in a dusty broken shoe—"and I'm dying on my feet wid hunger and the wakeness."

"Wait, then," I cried, on a sudden impulse.

"Go round to the front entrance.'

I hurried into the hall—intent on benevolence and broken victuals—and flung the door wide open. Quick as I had been, the tramp was already on the steps.

"Are they all out, miss?" he panted, in a husky voice.

"All," I replied, and I was about to add "except myself;" but ere I could utter another syllable he had sprung at me, seized me by the throat with brutal ferocity, and pressing me hard against a stone pillar, he proceeded to strangle me. I could not move, struggle, or scream. I felt his foul breath on my face, his savage, wolfish eyes fastened on mine. Everything was becoming black, the world reeled, a strange sound of the sea roared in my ears; I was suffocating, dying, dead! No, for here I awoke, and found myself sitting up and shrieking—shrieking like a maniac.

I saw Fanny jump out of bed by the light of a pale summer night, and come running over to me. She held me tightly, whilst I gasped and panted, precisely as if I had been really choked. Meantime all my relatives (in all sorts of costumes) poured into the room, believing (not unnaturally) that murder was being done.

Presently I recovered my voice, and in faint, broken sentences stammered out my tragic tale, which same tale was received with angry derision by father, and yells of laughter by my kindred. Robin, my eldest brother, who had been the first to arrive upon the scene, armed with an ancient horse pistol, was particularly indignant.

"If you are taken like this again, Cis, you will have to sleep in the far greenhouse, or in the back-yard; your yells sounded for all the world like a pig being killed."

Then, with as much dignity as was compatible with a pair of long bare legs and a short military cape, he made his exit

When all the kind inquirers had departed, I flung myself into Fanny's sympathetic arms, and enjoyed a thoroughly luxurious cry, and sobbed myself to sleep. "Cissy's friend with the red tie", and "Cissy's dream", became a sort of family joke and a byword with the boys for many, many months. At last other events thrust the jest into the background, and it was eventually forgotten, even by myself, though for weeks and weeks at night I had seemed to feel an iron grip upon my throat, and to meet in the dark the intolerable glare of a pair of wolfish eyes.

Two whole years had passed since I experienced that hideous vision. Robin was in India, with his regiment; Fanny was in Switzerland—on her honeymoon. We were quite a small party at home now—only five.

It was a lovely day in the month of September; father and every one of the family, also the servants, and almost every soul about the place, had departed at daybreak to the great annual fair, held at our nearest town. They had set out at three o'clock, and were not expected home until dark ; father had horses to sell and cattle to buy, and each of the domestics required something, for besides a market for multitudes of sheep and oxen, this fair boasted merry-go-rounds, shows and booths. No one remained, save the cook, who might reasonably have been exhibited as "the fat woman", Scanlan the butler, and myself. Scanlan was an ancient retainer, formerly father's soldier servant, an old bachelor, with a close fist, and a crusty temper, who still insisted on treating me as if I were but six years of age. I spent the long hours busily; I had presided at the breakfast by candle-light; it was not often that I had a day to myself totally undisturbed, and I made the most of it.

I wrote letters, mended garments, re-arranged the smoking-room (a daring liberty), made two family cakes, and gathered and arranged a quantity of flowers. Then I prepared to enjoy a well-earned rest—and *Oliver Twist*. I drew my chair into a French window in the drawing-room, and sat with my back to the light, thrilled by the murder of poor Nancy. My nerves were strung to their highest tension, as I followed the awful career of Bill Sikes; my silly little heart was beating tumultuously; a mere mouse in the wainscot had actually made me jump. Judge, then, of my feelings, when suddenly a black shadow fell across the page, and turning, I beheld the man of my dream—red necktie and all!

Yes, there he was; and—no, I was not asleep, I was wide awake. His hulking body leant heavily against the sash, his frowsy hat was pulled over his eyes, whilst his great hands fumbled awkwardly for the handle of the window. I fastened the bolt precipitately, glanced quickly at the other windows; thank God, they were all closed! I then screamed out—

"What do you want?"

"Is the colonel within?"

"No; he is out."

"I want to see him badly. I served under him"

"Wait," I cried. Then I darted across the room. I tore at the bell; how it clanged and reverberated through the empty lower regions! I held the door ajar, and saw as it were, unconsciously, a gaunt, slouching figure pass to the front at a shambling run.

Scanlan's well-drilled military step was—oh! what a sweet sound to me! I spoke to him, still holding the door, ready to fly at an instant's notice.

"There is a dreadful-looking man about, a tramp. Put the chain upon the hall door, and don't let him in," I cried out hysterically.

"All right, miss," replied Scanlan, departing with loud, leisurely footsteps. I heard him put up the chain and open the door with his usual flourish. Presently he closed it and came back, saying very peevishly—

"There's not a soul there, Miss Cissy. Ye were up early, and ye fell asleep without doubt and ye dreamt it."

"No, not this time," was my enigmatic answer. "I expect he is hidden in the laurels. Keep the door locked and barred, for Heaven's sake! and, Scanlan"—in my most coaxing key—"if you don't mind, would you sit in the hall till they come back. I—I—feel dreadfully nervous"

Scanlan had no sympathy with "nerves"; nevertheless, he remained within call, biding in the dining-room and library.

They—meaning the family and servants—returned about eight o'clock, all full of their day's doings and in the highest spirits; they discoursed volubly of their bargains in colts, yearlings, calves, ribbons, shawls—and even "ginger-bread husbands".

"And you, of course, saw no one; you stick at home, Cis," said my brother Ted.

"You have nothing to tell us?"

"You are mistaken for once," I answered, tremulously; "the tramp I dreamt about, called—the man with the red necktie."

"Well, that is news. Did he leave his card for me?"

"I did not go to receive him this time, as you may imagine," I continued, with ill-assumed composure. "I called Scanlan, and when he opened the door, there was no one to be seen!"

"You don't say so!" cried Teddy, sarcastically. "I should have been rather surprised if there was; you were dreaming again. How does old pipe-day like attending on your visionary callers? I thought he looked rather black."

"But it was no dream this time," I repeated. "I saw the tramp as plainly as I see you; the dream was a warning, and saved my life."

"Saved your grandmother! Upon my word. Cissy, it is getting serious, you and your visitor with the red tie;" and he roared with laughter, as rudely as any brother in Great Britain.

Nevertheless, the next morning, he and every one looked grave enough, when news was brought by Pat, the post-boy, that old Pat and Mrs. Kelly, who lived at that lonely spot, the Back Lodge, and were credited with considerable savings, had been found with their house pillaged, and their throats cut. Their spoons, watch, and money, had been carried off, although the poor old couple had evidently made a desperate struggle for their lives and property. The furniture was upset, and the walls splashed with blood. However, the only clue to the murderer's identity was part of a red woollen necktie, found in the dead woman's rigid clutch; the other half was subsequently picked up in the wood: but the tramp, its owner, was never seen again; no, not even in my dreams.

The De Grabrooke Monument

Charlotte Riddell

Chapter I.

You want to know why I do not care to look at pictures of our great cathedrals, why, indeed, the very name of cathedral fills me with a shivering terror. Well, I will tell you, though it is a story I do not much like to repeat.

Far away from London, hundreds of miles away, there is an old, old town, a town gray and worn with age, where the many gabled houses have high-peaked, red-tiled roofs, where the streets are narrow and the lanes tortuous, where the five arched bridge spanning a sluggish river is covered with lichens and tender cushions of emerald moss, a marvellous piece of colour when the sun shines warm and bright upon it.

I was born there, not quite in the town, but on its outskirts, in a pleasant house, that had its gardens sloping down to the river, and was well-shaded from the high road which it faced, by a high holly hedge and a line of interlacing lime trees planted inside. It was a lovely house, a rambling, old-fashioned mansion, that had once belonged to some great family—quaint, and homely, and picturesque—all covered over with roses and jasmine and honeysuckle, and clematis—the common white with the small star-like flowers which smells so sweet in the fine autumnal weather.

Out on the other side of the town—inland as we called it, to distinguish our district from that which lay away from the windings of the river—there resided a sister of my father's, a sister so much older, that while we were children we always fancied she must have been his mother. When quite a girl, she married the then agent of the De Grabrooke estates. A great match it was considered at the time, for Mr. Herington had a nice little property of his own, and was high in favour with Sir Roland de Grabrooke, who was at that time the reigning baronet.

Sir Roland died, and other baronets succeeded, but Mr. Herington still remained agent; and when, at length, he too died, my aunt was permitted to remain on at the cottage, not far from the northern entrance to Grabrooke, which is the admiration of every stranger who sees it, and is certainly the most beautiful house of its size, I ever beheld.

My aunt was elderly and childless, and as there were—I will not say too many of us at home—but a very sufficient number—few days passed without one or other of her nieces finding time to walk across Oldstone and out along the main London road to Grabrooke.

Sometimes—often, indeed, it chanced that when we stayed later, or the weather grew inclement, or my aunt had an unexpected visitor, we remained with her for the night—indeed, it had grown to be an understood thing if we did not return home before twilight, no one was to feel uneasy at our absence.

"Aunt Hilda had kept us," and we would return with a budget of news, and a hamper full of good things, driven sedately through Oldstone by Thomas, aunt's staid old servant, in her little phaeton, drawn by a fat, lazy pony, we could all of us remember so long as we could remember anything.

We had no mother, or perhaps so easy an arrangement might not have satisfied the home anxieties and proprieties. My father might well be excused if, when he came back at night, tired and fagged, one face, more or less, was scarcely noticed amongst the number at hand to greet him; and for the rest, every one in Oldstone knew every one else, and an adventure, whether agreeable or disagreeable, was the last thing likely to occur to any person living within the shadow of that cathedral town.

Unless, indeed, the cathedral itself fell down some day, and buried us all in its ruins. That calamity had been freely prophesied for years past, by great architects, who were at the trouble of travelling all the way from London, to tell the clerical and municipal authorities of Oldstone, that the building in which every inhabitant of Oldstone felt a pride was most insecure, and that it would cost a large sum of money to render it ordinarily safe.

For a short time after one of these visits, the more timid of the population eschewed the narrow paths which ran through the churchyard, and were wont to look about them nervously from their accustomed seats on Sunday; but ere long, finding that nothing happened—that the old building showed no more signs of tumbling about our ears than had been the case for years previously, they took courage again, and began to talk of the impertinence of persons who talked as if those who reared such a pile did not understand their business.

Great architects repair in these days to Oldstone, but merely in order to pay homage to the greater genius of one of their guild, who has restored the cathedral, and rendered it perfectly unrecognisable by any one who remembers the building in its olden state.

Cleaned it has been, inside and out. The marks left by Time's fingers are obliterated. It has been scraped; it has been swept and garnished. The dear old monuments look as spick and span, as bright and clean as if only just turned out of the stonemason's yard. Not an inscription now on any wall is difficult to decipher. He who runs may read all about the good folks who departed this life a few hundred years ago, all about their pedigree, their deeds of valour, the names of their wives, the number of their children. The brasses are rubbed up as bright as door-plates; the pavement looks as if it had just been hearth-stoned. The old glass in the windows stares in sullen amazement at the new; the organ loft has been swept away bodily, and you can see the whole building at a glance.

Not a scrap of mystery left about the place now. The secrets of every nook and corner have been laid bare by the hand of innovation; fancy has not a place left wherein to weave a web. The most nervous person might pace the nuns' gallery without fear, and the way to the leads is as safe as the pavements in the Close. I can remember when the traditions of the cathedral were things not to be lightly spoken of— rather they were legends it was considered most seemly only to hint of in the firelight, or to whisper concerning when the autumn evenings were growing chill and drear.

In the watches of the night I have awakened and thought of the cathedral standing solitary and mighty in the darkness, its massive towers rising to Heaven, its stones worn with the tread of men and women, whose very names were forgotten, its history interwoven with the history of the country, till I have grown so frightened with the pictures fancy drew, that I dare not even turn my head upon my pillow.

But in the daytime we—Alick and I—could be brave enough. Not even the sexton, who had no doubt once been young and active, though our memories were not long enough to recall him as otherwise than tottering and feeble, was not so well acquainted with all the ins and outs of the cathedral as we.

No dean of Oldstone, I am satisfied, ever knew half so much about the building as my brother and myself.

We had climbed the worn and slippery steps scores— ay, hundreds of times; we had crept along the nuns' gallery, unimpeded by rubbish, unappalled by danger; we had gone like cats over the leads, and looked down upon the houses in the Close, and taken bird's-eye views of the quaint old town and surrounding country; we had burrowed into the vaults, and on one occasion Alick penetrated so far into one of the subterranean passages, that in the firm belief he had died of suffocation, I was about to rush away and alarm the town, when he re-appeared, his clothes very much torn, and his face and hands begrimed with dirt, but otherwise none the worse for his adventure.

Oh! Alick, my brother, you can never return to tell me whether in that far-away land, where you were laid to rest, your thoughts turned with tender longing to dreamy Old-stone, with its softly flowing river and its grand cathedral, where hand clasped in hand we used, evening after evening, to stand in the dark nave, and listen while the organist practiced, and rolled out harmonies that never seemed to us quite the same when we heard them in the daylight and amongst the congregation.

But I must hurry on, or I shall never have space to tell you my story.

I was quite grown up, nearly twenty years old, and Alick had got his regimentals and was home with us for a few weeks before going to India, when one afternoon I went across to Grabrooke to visit Aunt Hilda. She wanted me to remain the night; she was in the mood for a long talk, and she had heaps to tell me, she said, about Sir Edwin De Grabrooke, who was having the Court done up, inside and out, before he brought home his bride.

"They say she is not a willing bride," went on my aunt, settling herself more comfortably in her easy-chair. "Poor little thing, she was attached, you know, to young Sir Clement, and I do think it is a sin and a shame for this marriage to be forced upon her."

"But perhaps she may be fond of Sir Edwin," I remarked, "if only out of gratitude for his kindness to his nephew."

Aunt Hilda was an elderly lady and privileged; moreover, she had always energetic ways of expressing herself. Consequently I was not so much surprised as might be supposed when, in answer to my innocent observation, she said—

"Fiddle-de-dee!"

"But, aunt," I persisted, "he was very kind to Sir Clement. I have heard papa say no father could have been more devoted. Who else would have nursed him in that dreadful fever?"

"I would," interrupted Mrs. Herington. "I offered to do it. I went up to the court myself for the purpose and saw that doctor who is such a non-such in Sir Edwin's opinion, and told him I—Hilda Herington—was not afraid of fever or of death, if either met me in the way of my duty, and that I would gladly nurse the youth, whose mother I had known and loved, and whom I had held in my arms when he was not a day old."

"It was like you, aunt," I said.

"It was not like me, child," she answered; "I was never a person to thrust myself forward, where no one wanted me, to offer help, except where I knew it would be appreciated. I could not tell then what made me do it, but I am sure now that it was the certainty I, and no one else, could save him urged me on. Well, he is gone, poor lad—and now Sir Edwin is to marry pretty Lily in his stead."

"Aunt," I said, "I must be going. I would not stay a night away from home while Alick is with us for any consideration. There will be plenty of nights and days too, when I can stop with, after he is gone—gone!"

And then I broke down. I burst into such a passion of tears, that my aunt, who, despite her brusque manner, was one of the kindest creatures that ever breathed, kissed and soothed and cooed over me; and then, putting on my shawl, and tying my bonnet-strings with her fair, withered hands, bade me run away home, and make haste, or I should find darkness surprising me.

It was getting late to be out—late, that is, for the autumn time of year; and I hurried along as my aunt had advised, lest evening should close in ere I reached Oldstone.

But fast as I walked, my thoughts travelled faster. They kept flitting hither and thither: now back to the De Grabrookes who were dead and gone, now forward to the future Lady De Grabrooke, whom I had known when we were children, and she, a tiny, golden-haired, blue-eyed mite, was called Clement's little wife.

It all came back as though not a day had passed since Sir Clement—he was Sir Clement from six years old—said to Lily, standing in my father's garden—

"Make haste and grow, Lily. They won't let me marry you unless you are as tall as Miss Atterton."

Miss Atterton was the dean's daughter, and five feet ten exact measurement; but the lad loved to tease golden hair and blue eyes.

And now Sir Clement was dead, and his uncle meant to marry Lily. In secret I had always admired Sir Edwin myself. His dark, set face—his cold, proud bearing—his curt address—his look of grave, settled determination—were far more attractive to my girlish fancy than Sir Clement's sunny face and boyish manner and cheery voice had ever been.

"Ah! how he must have loved his nephew," I considered, "to nurse him in that dreadful fever, and never to smile since his death."

Except Aunt Hilda, every one in Oldstone I think shared my opinion of Sir Edwin; and I had never before heard Mrs. Herington cast, even by implication, a doubt on the perfect amiability of Sir Edwin's character. Since his nephew's death he had been studiously kind to every one for whom Sir Clement entertained a preference; and it was entirely of his goodness that my aunt remained on at the Cottage, for which reason it seemed strange she should object to his marrying Lilian, or any other person he fancied.

But then Mrs. Herington always was a little odd, and no good purpose could be served by thinking about her likes and dislikes; besides, it was growing dusk, and if I did not hurry along still faster, I should find the cathedral closed, and have to make a long detour in consequence.

How it may be at Oldstone since the restoration I cannot tell, but in those days we used the cathedral as a short cut— just as one might a field-path—in at the north door, out at the south, or *vice versa*, if it suited our convenience. St. Paul's before the fire was not a more common thoroughfare than Oldstone Cathedral when Alick and I were young.

Panting and out of breath, I reached the north door as twilight was settling down over the town, and shrouding everything in the cathedral in gloom and mystery; but I had not time then to do more than glance around while I sped along the chancel and across the nave. There was not a creature apparently in the building but myself, and my footsteps rang out through the stillness the while I hurried over the stones, beneath which lay prelates and warriors, lord and ladies, and humbler persons, whose inscriptions were worn away, whose very names were forgotten, save by the Almighty.

I reached the south door: I could have found my way to it blindfolded, but there was some light in the nave, which found its way down from the long line of windows near the roof. Yes, there was the door, closed. I put my hand out and lifted the ponderous latch; *the door was locked.* Never before—never—had I known Jardin, the sexton, lock the south door before fastening the north. He lived in one of the streets leading to the river—one of the streets close to the Green—and it had hitherto been his invariable practice to secure the north door, and then hobble slowly across to the south—all on his way home.

But now it was locked, true enough; and if I could not reach the north door before Jardin made it fast, I should be in a pretty fix. You may be quite sure I did not waste any time knocking at the south door. I took up my dress, and ran as for my life back to the other entrance.

Just as I got to the screen dividing the chancel from the nave, I heard the door banged violently.

"Stop, stop, stop!" I cried—I shouted—but only the lonely echoes answered me. The north door was fast when I reached it, and though I hammered on the oak till my fingers were sore, and kicked upon the lower panels till the dead might almost have heard—Jardin made no sign.

"What shall I do?—oh! What shall I do?" I thought, standing there on the cold stones, with that iron-studded door between me and human companionship; and then, my dears, I did just what it has often fallen to my lot to do since—I bore it.

I submitted; when once I felt assured Jardin was really gone I beat the door no longer—I cried aloud no more.

"I shall have to stop here all night," I thought. "Aunt Hilda will think I am at home, and at home they will think I am with Aunt Hilda."

That was the position. There was not the slightest chance of any one coming to look for me; and if I shrieked myself hoarse, I knew my cries would never be heard.

Was I afraid? you ask.

Well, yes. Though I knew every inch of the cathedral as thoroughly as I knew our own house—though I could not be considered a coward, I was afraid—cruelly, mortally afraid.

Hitherto I had thought little enough about the dead lying all around and within the cathedral, filling the vaults below—mouldering away to dust beneath the stones of the nave.

In the insolence of our youth, Alick and I had often mocked at the gruesome effigies upon the tombs, and laughed over the Old World inscriptions; but, my word! when I came to be left alone among them in darkness I seemed to feel, my mood was the reverse of merry.

Oh! oh for the sound of a human voice, the touch of a living hand, the glimmer even of a taper! And then came a new horror to me—or rather an old horror in a new shape—some day I should be in just such a place—not for a night merely, but for all the days and nights till the Resurrection morn. I should be one of the silent army by which I was then encompassed—one of the forgotten dead—one of the lonely, lonely folks, sleeping as quietly in the darkness as in the sunlight.

If I had never felt before—and probably I never really had—the need of religion, the necessity for belief, I felt it then; words to which I paid little attention when read by the old dean, came back to ears with quite a new meaning, and I fell on my knees and prayed as throughout the twenty years of my life I had never prayed before.

When I raised my head and looked around me into the darkness, I knew that half my fear had departed. I was not alone—no, I felt that, though no human friend or relative was near, though no created being was at hand, I knew I was not left solitary; though there was no hand I could touch, no voice I could hear, no face I could see, I comprehended vaguely it might be—for the faith like the religion of youth is mostly vague—yet certainly—that no harm could come to me, that I was as safe all alone in the cathedral as I had ever been in my earthly father's house.

The hours went by—surely hours never seemed so long. I heard the quarters strike, the half hours, the hours. I thought of what they were doing at home—thought of my aunt sitting in her pretty drawing-room, of all the people in Oldstone, not one of whom guessed any person was locked up all alone in the great cathedral; and then my thoughts always drifted back to the dead by whom I was surrounded, and of whom I knew quite well I should never think carelessly and lightly again.

I tried to go to sleep—but I could not. I counted hundreds and thousands. I strove to recall all the heads of last Sunday's sermons, and recollect forgotten verses of the Psalms—but it was useless. The very darkness seemed to be awake. In broad daylight I had never felt my eyes so wide open as they were during the time I sat in Oldstone Cathedral whiling the weary hours away.

At length there came a light stealing into the building; faint and feeble at first, it grew stronger by degrees, till at length every object stood out clear and cold in the beams of the risen moon. The stalls, the bishop's throne, the pulpit, the organ put up so high, the tombs of abbots and barons; all these things were visible now to my outward eyes, as they had been to my mental vision during the vigil I had kept.

There was the great De Grabrooke monument, a pile against the wall—of cumbrous marble and rude sculpture—a huge tasteless monument which quite blocked up one window, and, yet large as it was, had not sufficed the love or ostentation of the family, for in a memorial chapel hard by, quite discernible from the seat I occupied, another tomb had been erected.

At the base of the larger monument, knelt a baronet, his wife and children; on the top of the tomb lay another baronet, his head resting on a stone pillow, a bible in his left hand crossed over his breast, a sword in his right stretched out stiff beside him.

As for Sir Clement, a memorial window was to be erected ere long in remembrance of his short life, but as yet the cathedral contained no record of him save the plate on his coffin-lid hidden away from sight in the deep vault beneath the chapel.

If the cathedral had been lonely and terrible in the darkness, it was ten times more lonely in the moonlight creeping down the walls and stealing along the aisles, penetrating into mysterious corners, and chasing lingering shadows round the tombs.

The silvery beams seemed to flit here and there and everywhere, now shining on the pipes of the organs, no glimmering through the stained glass of the great east window, now throwing white patches on the steps leading to the communion table, and now throwing themselves as if weary across the recumbent effigy of some forgotten prelate.

Up and down the aisles, dodging in and out amongst the arches and behind the pillars, darting with quick haste into the side chapels, peeping into the stalls, wandering like careless visitors hither and thither! Never since that night have I beheld the moonbeams without thinking of Oldstone Cathedral, and the shadows and the light playing at a weird game of hide and seek in the gloomy cloisters and the grand lovely nave.

There was a fascination I could not resist about the light and the scene, though both terrified me; and so I sat in a familiar corner, and looked and looked till my eyes ached, till my eyelids closed with very weariness.

Higher and higher rose the moon; slowly she sailed from east to west till she left the chancel in comparative darkness; but of all this I saw nothing, knew nothing. At length I was fast asleep—slumbering as deeply and soundly as though I had been lying in my white-curtained bed at home instead of being all alone in Oldstone Cathedral surrounded by the great and mighty dead.

Chapter II.

How long I slept I cannot tell, but, when with a start and a shiver I awoke, it was to find myself numbed and dazed in a darkness I could just discern, in a building which seemed to my scattered senses full of every known and unknown horror.

Yet I did not cry out—I knew that my lips uttered no sound—I made no frantic efforts to escape as one so often tries to do in dreams, as one sometimes actually does in the first moments of returning consciousness.

The terror of it instead of unchaining my voice laid an icy hand upon my mouth and kept me still and silent.

And then I was cold—never before or since have I been *so* cold. Not after a night's vigil by a sick bed, not at daybreak upon the sea, never have I felt such an intensity of cold as I did awakening to find myself solitary in that lonely pile.

"Will morning never come?" I thought; and then half reproachfully contrasted my conditions with that of the dear ones at home, feeling first angry at the idea of their comfortable safety, and then quite subdued when I considered the alarm and anxiety they would experience if they knew I was not at Aunt Hilda's.

Many a soldier lying wounded on a battle-field, many a sailor clinging to the shrouds of a doomed vessel, must, I think, have experienced the same transitions of feeling as those through which I passed that night.

Often I have wondered whether Alick—but there that tragedy was mercifully hidden in the future on the night when chilled to my very bones I sat in the darkness and prayed for the morning to dawn.

No, it was not fancy; I shut my eyes and opened them again; I lifted my hand and rubbed them stealthily, so stealthily that not even a mouse would have been disturbed by my movements.

I was wide awake, and it was not fancy! My senses were playing no tricks with me—my imagination was not cheating me with any optical delusion! I turned away my head, and then turned and looked again.

In the Grabrooke chapel there was a faint flickering light, which as I gazed, grew stronger.

At first a mere glimmer, it spread and spread, till I could see the great monument and the quaint old tomb.

It was not fire—I knew that well enough from the beginning, though I could not tell you how I knew it.

Just for a moment the idea crossed my mind that thieves might have been concealed in the chapel, pillagers of the dead about to commence their unholy work, and under this impression, I crouched down in my seat, and concealed myself behind the high oaken partition.

"They will kill me if they find me here," I considered; and I sank down in the stall a trembling icicle amongst the stools and hassocks, on the matting.

I am particular in telling you all these details that you may understand I made no mistake as to what I beheld afterwards.

The light increased; slowly but steadily the body of flame grew and grew, till I could see the vaulted roof, the beautiful aisles, the carving on the top of the columns, the tattered banners pendant from the walls. And then there came a sound as of many muffled footsteps and by degrees soft at first and as if at some distance, swelling in volume as it approached nearer, music, sad, stately, solemn, floated through the building—a requiem for the dead.

You will wonder that I kept my senses; but with the opening note of the mysterious music fear seemed to flee away, and sadness to take its place.

My eyes filled with tears; my heart thrilled with an exquisite melancholy. I covered my face with my hands and sobbed in silence as I had often done before at a soldier's funeral only with a subtler sense of sadness.

For this music was grander and more mournful than the "Dead March in Saul"; it was more touching than Mozart's "Requiem"; more heart-breaking than anything I had ever heard.

And it was produced from no instrument fashioned by man; above my head the mellow organ was dumb and silent, yet the air was full of the divine harmony so awfully majestic, and yet so replete with woe.

No longer in dread of wicked men, but with a shivering fear upon me of what I might behold I slowly lifted my head, and kneeling on the ground raised my eyes till they were on a level with the top of the pew.

What a sight met my gaze! The Grabrooke chapel was ablaze with lights; hundreds of tapers illumined the monument, the kneeling figures, and the time-stained tomb.

In the aisle stood a goodly company of the dead and gone—priest and warrior, abbot and crusader, sainted nun and courtly beauty. The mouth of the vault yawned wide and black, and gathered round and about it were the De Grabrookes of generations past; De Grabrookes who had died abroad, who had been drowned and buried in the great deep, who had been slain in battles, beheaded on Tower Hill, burned at the stake, turned their faces to the wall in their own familiar rooms and gathered up their feet in their beds ere passing into the broad eternity. Here they were all, habited once more in their earthly robes of flesh, waiting, I could see, for one who tarried in the coming.

The chiefest among them carried torches, and, as I gazed, they formed into procession, and advanced to a small door beside the monument, which had in former days given private access to the De Grabrooke chapel. Many a mourner must in the times departed have come in by that door to pray, but I had never seen it opened, not even when Sir Clement was borne to his last resting-place. The hinges were stiff, the bolts red with rust, no key would have turned in the massive lock. The armour in the hall at Grabrooke Court did not seem less necessary to the family now than that heavy door which once swung wide so easily, and yet it was towards this door the ghostly company pressed forward—the while the music rose and fell died away almost to a whisper, and then wailed out in louder notes of woe.

There was one I had known among the De Grabrookes missing—young Sir Clement. With a terrified curiosity my eyes looked for him without much success.

They waited—but I could see they were growing impatient. Though there was no speech nor voice amongst them, I knew they were all swayed by a common purpose—that they had gathered together to confront someone who ought to have been there ere now.

"He is coming!"

I heard the words distinctly—as distinctly as I heard the sobbing wail of the mysterious music, and yet none of the De Grabrookes uttered them; rather the sound seemed to come from a far away part of the cathedral.

"He is coming!" and there was a stir of expectation, a thrill of human emotion amongst the dead men and the dead women.

"Buried at night," was almost whispered in my ear. Turning suddenly, I tried to see who spoke, but there was no one near me.

At that moment there came a blast of keen, cold air through the cathedral; the torches flickered and the flames waved with the force of the wind which rushed in through the open door of the De Grabrooke chapel.

That door stood wide; through it I could see the graves in the Cathedral yard, the railings round the tombs, the tress in the green, the canon's houses on the other side the road.

Quick, quick, up the flagged path leading to the door so long disused, came a man hurrying fast; his footsteps rung out on the stones. Looking neither to right nor to left, he strode to meet awful company.

It was he they had expected—he they were waiting for; and he was coming, he was at hand.

They all pressed forward as he entered—a terrible band—all men, women, and children. He sped thither in hot haste, of that there could be no question; his dress was careless, his looks wild, his hair in disorder, and as he took off his hat when he passed through the door, I could see his face looked ghastly as if one in the throes of some mortal agony or terror.

From his brow he wiped the moisture which gathered there, and would have passed on towards the vault, but that the De Grabrooke dead gathered together and prevented him.

He looked at them each individually, and then around.
It was Sir Edwin De Grabrooke!

I thought I must have shrieked aloud. The light of the tapers fell full upon him as he stood there repulsed. The dead did not look more corpselike than he; the countenances of the dead were not more terrible in their rigid sternness, than his in its desperate defiance.

Once again he made a movement as if to pass on towards the open vault, and again the silent dead barred his passage.

Then in a moment they drew back forming on each side in line, and leaving a path wide enough for him to have pushed on had he chosen to do so.

But he did not so choose, rather he stood rooted to the spot, gazing at a figure which issued from the vault and came slowly towards him.

Sir Clement—robed not in any garments he had worn in life, but with his grave clothes draped about him; Sir Clement—with a look of sorrowful reproach in his young eyes; Sir Clement for whom all the other dead made way—falling aside and behind till he and his kinsman stood face to face.

Great as was my fear, my curiosity was greater. I slipped from my place and crossed the aisle and crept along, keeping well in the shade till I could hide myself behind what we called the King's Tomb, as there was a tradition that some Danish monarch lay mouldering there.

Scarcely venturing to draw my breath—though not one of the ghostly throng had a thought to spare for me—I peeped from between an angel's wings and beheld the uncle and the nephew standing still, the one confronting the other in a silence more appalling than the wildest tumult.

Slowly the dead youth bared his heart, and drawing it open a ghastly spectacle disclosed a sharp long weapon, fine as a needle, fatal as the cruellest sword, which penetrated it through and through.

The grave had given up its secrets; only a morsel of steel; only a human life; only one who had stood between sent in a moment to his long account; and now, all the dead De Grabrookes had risen to drive out the traitor from amongst them.

There was a sound as of a rising storm, as of a gathering tempest, and while one wild blast swept round the cathedral, they thrust him out into the night, and with skeleton hands closed and bolted the door behind.

Then there came utter darkness.

Chapter III.

For weeks I hovered on the borderland. Now the doctors told the dear ones who moved about my bed that it must be death; then a slight change for the better gave them hope, and they said it was possible I might live.

I had been found in the early morning by the organist of the cathedral, lying insensible on the cold pavement beside the King's Tomb. From the cathedral I was carried into the Deanery close at hand, and then, the doctors having pronounced that life was not extinct, my father insisted on taking me home, where Aunt Hilda came to help in the weary nursing which followed.

Of all these details I remembered not one. My memory was a complete black from the time the De Grabrooke chapel door was shut till I came back, after weeks of mortal sickness, to the knowledge that I was still alive, that the weak, wan, helpless creature who lay back on the pillows, was the shadow of the robust, lighthearted girl who had walked into Oldstone Cathedral strong and well to be carried out of it fourteen hours later a mere wreck of her former self.

When I could speak connectedly I did not tell of what I had seen during the course of that awful night. In all the years which have come and gone since then I have never told the story right through until to-night. During my illness I had raved of terrible things, reproducing doubtless the horrors my eyes had witnessed, but those around me attributed all I said to delirium.

"The terror of finding herself shut up in the cathedral was too much for her," declared my relatives, and Oldstone echoed this opinion.

"I am quite sure, Patty, you were not well when you left me that night," said Aunt Hilda, who never ceased searching about for natural causes to account for my illness. I did not contradict her. I knew she desired to believe there was nothing at the bottom of the wild ravings she had listened to, and so I held my peace. Only once, when a visitor marked in my presence that Lily's wedding was to be in the spring, I spoke out suddenly, and declared, "Oh! she must not marry Sir Edwin; she must not."

Then my aunt signed to her friend to be silent, and turning to me entreated that I would keep myself quite quiet.

"You will begin to wander again, Patty, if you excite yourself," she added.

This was how they managed, and they treated me one and all so judiciously, I declare at length the memory of that night came to be merely as the memory of some bad dream. Before the crocuses and the snowdrops peeped through the bare earth, I learned to regard the visions I had seen as a part of my delirium, as one of the many terrible pageants at which I had assisted, while my flesh and my spirit fought out their battle as to whether they were then to part company or remain together for years to come.

All this time Alick, for whose sake I had hurried home from Aunt Hilda's snug little bower, was still in England. At the eleventh hour some alteration had taken place in the minds of those who rule at the Horse Guards, and orders were sent countermanding the departure of his regiment when it was almost on the eve of embarkation.

Thus it came to pass he was able to spend Christmas with us, and when May came—May with all its sweet airs and lovely blossoms—he was at Oldstone once again, this time paying really his last visit, for he sailed two months afterwards, and—but that has nothing to do with this story.

It was May, then, and Alick and I were wandering after breakfast up and down the walk beside the river, he laughing and merry, I more quiet than had been my wont before that long exhausting, illness, but serenely happy in his companionship, and rejoicing, as who does not rejoice in the sights and sounds of spring.

It was a perfect morning, the blue heaven was reflected in the water gliding past us, the scent of the hawthorn came wafted from the bushes growing on the opposite bank of the river. Our own garden was a mass of flowers, and I who, had been almost dead, was alive again, able to walk amid all this beauty, and thank God for the comparative strength and health He had restored to me.

"What an exquisite day," I said, as we stood looking at the sunshine lying across fields where cattle were lazily grazing.

"Yes. Lily could not have had a more delicious morning for her wedding, could she?"

"Lily!" I repeated, "What do you mean, Alick?"

He laughed and coloured.

"By the by, I ought not to have mentioned the matter. We were all bound over to silence, but I quite forgot Aunt Hilda's injunction. She thought you had better hear nothing about the marriage till it was over and done with."

"Because of what I said when I was delirious, I suppose?" I remarked, thoughtfully. "Certainly I had the strangest notions."

"Do not think of them," he entreated. "We cannot have you laid up again, Patty."

We took a few turns in silence, then I said, "Alick, I would give the world to have just one peep at Lily as a bride."

He shook his head.

"You are not strong enough yet, little woman, to go sight-seeing."

"But I am strong," I persisted, "as strong as I ever shall be again; and it will do me no harm to cross my fancy; I feel it will, Alick. You know the doctors said I was to have everything I asked for."

Alick laughed outright, mine was such barefaced casuistry, but again negatived my proposition.

"You must not think of it, dear," he said in his kind, loving way. "I am quite sure you have had enough of the cathedral to last you for the remainder of your natural life."

Still I persisted—insisted rather. I could give fifty reasons for my desire where he could only give one against it, and so at length I gained my point, all the more readily, perhaps, because he was at heart as eager as I to see the show.

"We will not try though to get in amongst the crowd," he bargained. "All Oldstone is certain to be there, and you are not fit to be hustled about or stared at by the good people in the town. We will just go round the cloisters, and steal through our own particular little door, and get up into the nuns' gallery, and we shall see everything there, and nobody be a bit wiser."

Entering at the most remote gate, and creeping our way in and out amongst the tombs and headstones, we reached the cloisters, which were quite deserted, and surreptitiously made our way high up to a point where, without being seen, we could obtain a view of the whole of the proceedings.

The cathedral was full—full to overflowing. Every available seat was occupied. People in the aisles were craning their heads over the shoulders of those in front of them. Only one passage, and that the principal one, was kept clear for the bridal party. We could not have obtained standing-room had we tried our chance amongst the crowd.

The sun was shining in through the windows, stained and unstained. It was the brightest of all bright sights to look down from our eyrie—and see the ladies' dresses—and the lovely flowers—and the rich colours cast by the old glass. Everything seemed so bright, so gay that for the time I quite forgot myself—forgot I had ever spent a night alone in the cathedral—and that I had there either dreamed strange dreams, or beheld terrible visions.

"Why, I believe coming has done you good," said my brother in a low voice, surveying me with wondering eyes. "You look quite bright and cheerful, Patty."

For answer I only squeezed his fingers, and then began to pick out our most intimate friends from amidst the spectators.

"Do you see Miss Atterton, Alick?" I whispered; "she has got a new bonnet; and see, there is aunt, and Mrs. James Herington, and Nina Lovelace, is not she pretty! And look, Alick—"

"Hist!" he interposed. "Here they come."

Yes, there they came. In a minute more they were ranged before the altar, and the dean began the service.

I could not take my eyes off Lily, she was as white as her floral namesake, and there was a look in her face I had never before seen in any living face, and that I trust I may never see again.

In a moment all the brightness and sunshine seemed to fade away, leaving nothing save a dull darkness before my eyes. The goodly company, the many coloured dresses, the delicate flowers vanished, and in their places there came desolation and silence, save for the voice of the dean beginning "Dearly beloved."

"Alick, I am afraid I am going to be ill—I feel very faint!" I gasped.

"For mercy's sake, Patty, keep up for a little, we can't get away without making some noise, and one might almost hear a pin drop below. Have you not some smelling-salts with you?"

I had, and with a great effort kept myself up, figuratively, as he desired. I leaned my hand against the rough wall behind me, and tried to steady the objects in the cathedral which would keep slipping, slipping from my sight.

At intervals I could see distinctly Sir Edwin's dark face, and Lily's so ghastly, ghastly white, the evil countenance of the doctor who had attended Sir Clement in his last illness, and then they would all blend with the figures kneeling before the De Grabrooke monument, with the stiff effigy on the De Grabrooke tomb.

"Into which holy estate," proceeded the dean, "these two persons present come now to be joined. Therefore, if any man can show any just cause why they may not lawfully be joined together, let him now speak, or else hereafter for ever hold his peace."

"I can. He is a murderer!"

The words rang out through the ancient edifice clear as a bell, and echoed along the roof of the cathedral, as if the sentence were taken up and repeated by fifty voices. In a moment all was confusion, every one seemed to be moving, hundreds of people appeared to be pressing forward to one spot, a thousand colours danced before my eyes, a hum as of a multitude of people talking sounded in my ears; then I felt myself hurried along, dragged down the dark steep broken steps, and so breathless out into the open air.

"*I* did not speak, Alick!" I cried. "*I* said nothing!"

His face and clothes were covered with dust and dirt, he was panting as if he had run a race, drops of perspiration were on his forehead, but he did not answer a word.

He took me in his arms and keeping well out of sight till we were clear of the Close, struck into a narrow passage between two blank walls.

Then he put me to the ground and catching my hand said—

"Run, Patty! Whether you are able to or not, you must run now."

I do not know how I did it. I cannot imagine how my limbs so weak and feeble carried me along, but at last we were safe—quite safe on the bank of our own tranquil river, and we had not met a creature by the way.

How long we sat there I do not know—not very long, I daresay, though it seemed hours to me.

As well as he could Alick brushed the cobwebs and dirt from his clothes, and washed his hands and face in the river, then with very pale cheeks he turned to and said—

"Patty, we will get home now; we can go through the garden, and you must lie down in your own room. I will return to the town and see what has happened; but remember one thing, to no human being, not to father or aunt, or anyone else, must you confess we were in the cathedral this day: you understand me, dear?"

His tone was very tender and pitiful, though his words were so urgent.

For answer I held out my hands and began to cry.

"*I* did not speak, Alick. I assure you I did not say a word."

"Never mind that, dear," he answered, kissing me still with the same sorrowful tenderness; "only keep your own counsel and I will keep it too."

I had another illness. Whatever my ravings revealed, or my family suspected, was kept so close a secret that not a creature in Oldstone guessed Alick and I had been in the nuns' gallery when the dean's exhortation met with so fearful a response.

Before I could leave my room Alick had to say good-by in reality.

It was one evening at twilight he came to part with me, and we sat for a while hand clasped in hand in total silence, our hearts too full for speech.

At last he said—

"Patty, before I go to India there is something I want to tell you. No one else will, perhaps, and you may hear it suddenly."

"About—about—I understand," I exclaimed feebly.

"Yes, about that morning. Even father does not know for certain that we were there."

"I am glad of it," I said.

"The marriage did not go on," he proceeded after a pause.

"Not then?" I asked.

"Not ever," he answered; "it will never take place now."

I raised myself on my elbow and tried to see his face, for his tone implied more even than his words, but it was too dark for me to distinguish his features.

"Sir Edwin had a fit!" he went on speaking, slowly and cautiously.

"Yes?" I said, interrogatively.

"And somehow—we cannot tell how such things grow—there got about a belief that Sir Clement did not die of fever—that he came to his end unfairly. Do you feel faint, Patty?"

"No, go on. I would rather hear it from you."

"Well, at last there was such a fuss made that an order came for the body to be exhumed."

"You need not go on," I said. "I know—I know—I know. It was not delirium then, Alick, it was truth?"

"It was truth," he answered.

"And Sir Edwin?" I asked, half-afraid to enquire, and yet feeling that I must put the question.

"Sir Edwin destroyed himself; that is what most of all I wanted to tell you."

"And was he buried in the De Grabrooke vault?"

Alick hesitated a minute, but then replied—

"No, he was buried in another place at midnight. Now, Patty, you know everything."

That is the story, my dears, and we will talk no more about it.

A Vanished Hand

Clotilde Graves

"Why," Daymond wrote, "*do you imagine that I shall despise you for this confession? None but a whole-souled, high-hearted woman could have made it! You have said you love me, frankly; and I say in return that had the fountains of my heart not been hopelessly dried up at their sources, they must have sprung forth gladly at such words from you. But the passion of love, dear friend, it is for me no more to know; and I hold you in too warm regard to offer you, in exchange for shekels of pure Ophir gold, a defaced and worthless coinage!*"

As Daymond penned the closing words of the sentence, the last rays of the smoky-red London sunset were withdrawn. Only a little while ago he had replenished the fire with fresh logs; but they were damp, and charred slowly, giving forth no pleasant flame. He struck a match and lighted a taper that stood upon his writing table. It created a feeble oasis of yellow radiance upon the darkness of the great studio, and the shadow of Daymond's head and shoulders bending above it, was cast upward in gigantesque caricature upon the skylight, reduced to frosty white opacity by a burden of March snow.

Daymond poised the drying pen in white, well-kept fingers, and read over what he had written. Underlying all the elegance of well-modelled phrases was the sheer brutality of rejection, definitely expressed. His finely strung mental organisation revolted painfully at the imperative necessity of being cruel.

"She asks for bread," he cried aloud, "and I am giving her a stone!" The lofty walls and domed roof of his workshop gave back the words to him, and his sensitive ear noted the theatrical twang of the echo. Yet the pang of remorse that had moved him to speech was quite genuine.

"You have heard my story," he wrote on.

A great many people had heard it, and had been bored by it; but, sensitive as Daymond's perceptions were, he was not alive to this fact.

"Seventeen years ago, while I was still a student dreaming of fame in a draughty Paris studio, I met the woman who was destined—I felt it then as I know it now—to be the one love of my life. She was an American, a little older than myself. She was divinely beautiful to me—I hardly know whether she was really so or not. We gave up all, each for each. She left husband, home, friends, to devote her life to me. I—"

He paused, trying to sum up the list of his own sacrifices, and ultimately left the break, as potent to express much, and went on:

"Guilty as I suppose we were, we were happy together—how happy I dare not even recall. Twenty-four months our life together lasted, and then came the end. It was the cholera year in Paris; the year which brought me my first foretaste of success in Art, robbed me of all joy in life . . . She died. Horribly! suddenly! And the best of me lies buried in her grave!"

The muscles of his throat tightened with the rigor that accompanies emotion; his eyelids smarted. He threw back his still handsome head, and a tear fell shining on the delicately scented paper underneath his hand. He looked at the drop as it spread and soaked into a damp little circle, and made no use of the blotting paper to remove the stain.

If any crudely candid observer had told Daymond that he dandled this desolation of his—took an aesthetic delight in his devotion to the coffined handful of dust that had once lived and palpitated at his touch, he would have been honestly outraged and surprised. Yet the thing was true. He had made his sorrow into a hobby-horse during the last fifteen years of honest regret, of absolute faithfulness to the memory of his dead mistress. It gratified him to see the well-trained creature dance and perform the tricks of the *haute école.* He was aware that the romance of that past, which he regretted with such real sincerity, added something to the glamour of his achieved reputation, his established fame, in the eyes of the world. The halo which it cast about him had increased his desirability in the eyes of the great lady who, after affording him numberless unutilised opportunities for the declaration of a sentiment which her large handsome person and her large handsome property had inspired in many other men, had written him a frank, womanly letter, placing these unreservedly at his disposal . . . And Daymond, in his conscious fidelity and unconscious vanity, must perforce reply wintrily, nipping with the east wind of non-reciprocity the mature passion tendrils which sought to twine themselves about him. It was a painful task, though the obligation of it tickled him agreeably—another proof of the inconsistency of the man, who may be regarded as a type of humanity; for we are all veritable Daymonds, in that the medium which gives us back to our own gloating eyes day by day is never the crystal mirror of Truth, but such a lying glass as the charlatans of centuries agone were wont to make for ancient Kings and withered Queens to mop and mow in.

Daymond pushed back his chair, and got up, and began to pace from end to end of the studio. The costly Moorish carpets muffled the falling of his footsteps, which intermittently sounded on the polished interspaces of the parqueted floor, and then were lost again in velvet silence. In the same way, his tall figure, with its thoughtfully bending head and hands clasped behind it, would be swallowed up among the looming shadows of tall easels or faintly glimmering suggestions of sculptured figures which here and there thrust portions of limbs, or angles of faces, out of the dusk—to appear again with the twilit north window for its background, or emerge once more upon the borders of the little island of taper-shine. So he moved amid the works of his genius restlessly and wearily to and fro; and the incoherent mutterings which broke from him showed that his thoughts were running, in the beaten track of years.

"If I could see her again—if our eyes and lips and hands and hearts might meet for even the fraction of a minute, as they used to do, it would be enough. I could wait then patiently through the slow decay of the cycles for the turning of the key in the rusty wards, and the clanking of my broken fetters on the echoing stone, and the burst of light that shall herald my deliverance from prison! . . . " He lifted his arms above his head. "Oh, my dead love, my dear love! if you are near, as I have sometimes fancied you were, speak to me, touch me—once, only once! . . ." He waited a moment with closed eyelids and outstretched hands, and then, with a dry sob of baffled longing, stumbled back to his writing table, where the little taper was flickering its last, and dropped into his arm-chair.

"And other women talk of love to me. What wonder I am cold as ice to them, remembering her!"

It was a scene he had gone through scores upon scores of times—words and gestures varying according to the pathetic inspiration of the moment. He knew that he was pale, and that his eyes were bleared with weeping, and he had a kind of triumph in the knowledge that the pain of retrospective longing and of present loneliness was so poignantly real and keen. Out of the blackness behind his chair at that moment came a slight stir and rustle—not the sough of a vagrant draught stirring among folds of tapestry, but an undeniably human sound. But half displeased with the suspicion that there had been a witness to his agony, he turned—turned and saw Her, the well-beloved of the old, old time, standing very near him.

Beyond a vivid sensation of astonishment, he felt little. He did not tremble with fear—what was there in that perfectly familiar face to fear? He did not fall, stammering with incoherent rapture, at her feet. And yet, a few moments ago, he had felt that for one such sight of her, returned from the Unknowable to comfort him—dragged back from the mysterious Beyond by his strong yearnings—he would have bartered fame, honour, and wealth—submitted his body to unheard-of tortures—shed his blood to the last heart's drop. He had prayed that a miracle might be performed—and the prayer had been granted. He had longed—desperately longed—to look on her once more—and the longing was satisfied. And he could only stare wide-eyed, and gape with dropped jaw, and say stupidly:

"You?"

For answer she turned her face—in hue, and line, and feature, no one whit altered—so that the light might illumine it fully, and stood so regarding him in silence. Every pore of her seemed to drink in the sight of him;—her lips were parted in breathless expectancy. Every hair of the dark head—dressed in the fashion of fifteen years ago; every fold of the loose dress she wore—a garment he knew again; every lift and fall of her bosom seemed to cry out dumbly to him. There was a half-quenched spark glimmering in each of her deep eyes, that might have wanted only one breath from his mouth to break out into flame. Her hands hung clasped before her. It seemed as if they were only waiting for the signal to unclasp—for the outspread arms to summon him to her heart again. But the signal did not come. He caught a breath, and repeated, dully:

"You! It is you?"

She returned:

"It is I!"

The well-known tones! Recollection upsprang in his heart like a gush of icy waters. For a moment he was thrilled to the centre of his being. But the smitten nerve chords ceased to vibrate in another moment, and he rose to offer her a chair.

She moved across and took it, as he placed it by the angle of the wide hearth; and lifted her skirts aside with a movement that came back to him from a long way off, like her tone in speaking—and, shading her deep grey eyes from the dull red heat with her white left hand, looked at him intently. He, having pushed his own seat back into the borders of the shadowland beyond the taper's gleam and the hearth glow, looked back at her. That hand of hers bore no ring. When he had broken the plain gold link that had fettered it in time past, he had set in its place a ruby that had belonged to his mother. The ruby was on his finger now. He hid it out of sight in the pocket of his velvet painting coat, not knowing why he did so. And at that moment she broke the silence with:

"You see I have come to you at last!"

He replied, with conscious heaviness:

"Yes—I see!"

"Has the time seemed long? . . . We have no time, you know, where . . . Is it many days since? . . . "

"Many days!"

"My poor Robert! . . . Weeks? . . . Months? . . . Not years? . . . "

"Fifteen years . . . "

"Fifteen years! And you have suffered all that time. Oh, cruel! cruel! If there was more light here, I might see your face more plainly. Dear face! I shall not love it less if there are lines and marks of grief upon it—it will not seem less handsome to me at forty than it did at twenty-five! Ah, I wish there was more light!" The old pettishly coaxing tones! "But yet I do not wish for it, lest it should show you any change in *me*!"

"You are not changed in the least." He drew breath hard. "It might be yesterday—," he said, and left the sentence unfinished.

"I am glad," said the voice that he had been wont to recall to memory as wooingly sweet. "They have been kinder than I knew . . . Oh! it has always been so painful to recall," she went on, with the old little half shrug, half shudder, "that I died an *ugly* death—that I was not pretty to look at as I lay in my coffin! . . . "

Daymond recoiled inwardly. That vanity, in a woman, should not be eradicated by the fact of her having simply ceased to exist, was an hypothesis never before administered for his mental digestion.

"How curiously it all happened," she said, her full tones trembling a little. "It was autumn—do you remember?— and the trees in the Bois and the gardens of the Luxembourg were getting yellowy brown. There were well-dressed crowds walking on the Boulevards, and sitting round the little tables outside the restaurants. One could smell chloride of lime and carbolic acid crossing the gutters, and see the braziers burning at the corners of infected streets, and long strings of hearses going by; but nothing seemed so unlikely as that either of us should be taken ill and die. We were too wicked, you said, and too happy! . . . only the good, miserable people were carried off, because any other world would be more suitable to them than this . . .

It was nonsense, of course, but it served us to laugh at. Then, because you could not sell your great Salon picture, and we could not afford the expense, you gave a supper at the *Café des Trois Oiseaux* (*Cabinet particulier No. 6*)—and Valéry and the others joined us. I was so happy that night . . . my new dress became me . . . I wore yellow roses—your favourite Maréchal Niel's. When I was putting them in my bosom and my hair you came behind and kissed me on the shoulder. *O, mon Dieu! mon Dieu!* I can feel it now! We went to the Variétés, and then to supper. I had never felt so gay. People are like that, I remember having heard, just when they are going to die. Valéry gaped—I believe he was half in love with me—and I teased him because I knew you would be jealous. In those days you would have been jealous of the studio écorché. Ha! ha! ha!"

Daymond shuddered. The recurrent French phrases jarred on him; something in her voice and manner scarified inexpressibly his sensitive perceptions. He wondered, dumbly, whether she had always been like this? She went on:

"And then, suddenly, in the midst of the laughter, the champagne, the good dishes—the pains of hell!" She shuddered. "And then a blank, and waking up in bed at the hospital, still in those tortures—and getting worse and seeing in your white face that I was going to die! Drip-drip! I could feel your tears falling upon my face, upon my hand; but I was even impatient of you in my pain. Once I fancied that I heard myself saying that I hated you. Did I really?"

"I think—I believe you did! But, of course—" Daymond stopped, and shuddered to the marrow as she leaned across to him caressingly, so near that her draperies brushed his knee and her breath fanned upon his face.

"Imagine it!" she cried, "that I *hated* you! *You* to whom I had given myself—you for whom I left my—"

He interrupted, speaking in an odd, strained voice: "Never mind that now."

"I had always wished to die first," she resumed, "but not in that way; not without leaving you a legacy of kind words and kisses. Ah!" (her voice stole to his ears most pleadingly), "do you know that I have been here, I cannot tell how long, and you have not kissed me once, darling?"

She rose up in her place—she would have come to him, but he sprang to his feet, and thrust out both hands to keep her off, crying:

"No! no!"

She sank back into her seat, looking at him wide-eyed and wonderingly. "Is he afraid of me?" she whispered to herself.

"I am not afraid of you," Daymond returned almost roughly. "But you must make allowances for me at first. Your sudden coming—the surprise—"

"Ah yes! the surprise—and the joy—?"

He cleared his throat and looked another way. He was shamedly conscious that the emotion that stiffened his tongue and hampered his gestures was something widely different from joy. He spoke again, confusedly. "This seems like old times—before—"

"Before I died," she said, "without bidding good-bye to you. Dear! if you guessed how I have longed to know what you said and did when it was all over, you would not mind telling me . . . *Are they grieving—those whom I have left behind?*' is a question that is often asked in the place I come from. You were sorry? You cried? Ah! I know you must have cried!"

"I believe," Daymond returned, moving restlessly in his chair, "that I did. And I—I kissed you, though the doctors told me not to. I wanted to catch the cholera and die, too, I believe! . . . "

"Yes?"

"And when the people came with—the coffin, I"—he bit his lip—"I would not let them touch you! . . . "

"My poor boy!"

He winced from the tenderness. He felt with indescribable sensations the light pressure of that well-known once well-loved touch upon his arm.

"And then—after the funeral, I believe I had a brain fever." He passed his hand through his waving, slightly grizzled hair, as if to assist his lagging memory—really, as an excuse for shaking off that intolerable burden of her hand. "And when I recovered I found there was no way to forgetfulness"—he heard her sigh faintly—"except through work. I worked then—I am working still."

"Always alone?"

"Generally alone. I have never married."

"Of course not!"

A faint dissent began to stir in him at this matter-of-fact acquiescence in his widowed turtle-like celibacy. "It may interest you to know," he observed, with a touch of the pompous manner which had grown upon him with the growth of his reputation, "that my career has been successful in the strongest sense of the word. I became, I may say, one of the leaders of the world of Art. Upon the decease or resignation of the President of the ——, it is more than probable that I shall be invited to occupy his vacant place. And an intimation has reached me, from certain eminent quarters"—he paused weightily—"that a baronetcy will be conferred upon me, in that event!"

"Yes?"

The tone betrayed an absolute lack of attention. She had once been used to take a keen interest in his occupations; to be cast down by his failures and elated by his successes. Had that enthusiasm constituted the greater part of her charm? In its absence Daymond began to find her—must it be confessed?—but indifferent company.

In the embarrassment that momentarily stiffened him, an old habit came to his rescue. Before he knew it, he had taken a cigar from a silver box upon the writing table, and was saying, with the politely apologetic accent of the would-be smoker:

"May I? You used not to mind!"

She made a gesture of assent. As the first rings of bluish vapour mounted into the air, Daymond found her watching him with those intent, expectant eyes.

Feeling himself bound to make some observation, he said: "It is very wonderful to me to see you here! It was very good of you to come!"

She returned: "They had to let me come, I think! I begged so—I prayed so, that at last—" She paused. Daymond was not listening. He was looking at her steadfastly and pondering . . .

It had been his whim, in the first poignancy of bereavement, to destroy all portraits of her, so that with the lapse of years no faulty touch should betray the memory of her vanished beauty. It struck him now for the first time that his brush had played the courtier, and flattered her, for the most part, unblushingly. He found himself criticising unfavourably the turn of her throat and the swell of her bosom, and the dark voluptuous languishment of her look. The faint perfume of heliotrope that was shaken forth now, as of old time, from her hair and her garments no longer intoxicated, but sickened him. This, then, was the woman he had mourned for fifteen years! He began to feel that he had murmured unwisely at the dispensation of Providence. He began to revolt at this recrudescence of an outworn passion—to realise that at twenty-five he had taken a commonplace woman for a divinity—a woman whom, if she had not died when she did, he would have wearied of—ended perhaps in hating. He found himself in danger of hating her now.

"At last they let me come. They said I should repent it—as if I could!" Her eyes rested on him lingeringly; her hand stilled the eager trembling of her lips. "Never! Of course, you seemed a little strange at first. You are not quite—not quite yourself now; it is natural—after fifteen years. And presently, when I tell you—Oh! what will you say when I tell you all?"

She left her chair and came toward him, so swiftly that he had not time to avoid her. She laid her hand on his shoulder and bent her mouth to his ear. One of her peculiarities had been that her lips were always cold, even when her passion burned most fiercely. The nearness of those lips, once so maddeningly desirable and sweet, made Daymond's flesh creep horribly. He breathed with difficulty, and the great drops of agony stood thickly on his forehead—not with weak, superstitious terror of the ghost; with unutterable loathing of the woman.

"Listen!" she said. "They are wise in the place I came from; they know things that are not known here . . . You have heard it said that once in the life of every human being living upon earth comes a time when the utterance of a wish will be followed by its fulfilment. The poor might be made rich, the sick well, the sad merry, the loveless beloved—in one moment—if they could only know when that moment comes! But not once in a million million lifetimes do they hit upon it; and so they live penniless and in pain, and sorrowful and lonely, all their lives. I let my chance go by, like many others, long before I died; but yours is yet to come." Her voice thrilled with a note of wild triumph; the clasp of her arm tightened on his neck. "Oh, love!" she cried; "the wonderful moment is close at hand! It is midnight now"— she pointed to the great north window, through which the frosty silver face of the moon was staring in relief against a framed-in square of velvet blackness, studded with twinkling star-points—"but with the first signs of the dawn that you and I have greeted together, heart of my heart!—how many times in the days that may come again!—with the graying of the East and the paling of the stars comes the Opportunity for you. Now, do you understand?"

He understood and quailed before her. But she was blindly confident in his truth, stupidly reliant on his constancy.

"When it comes, beloved, you shall take me in your arms—breathe your wish upon these lips of mine, in a kiss. Say, while God's ear is open, 'Father, give her back to me, living and loving, as of old!' and I shall be given—I shall be given!"

She threw both arms about him and leaned to him, and sobbed and laughed with the rapture of her revelation and the anticipation of the joy that was to come.

"Remember, you must not hesitate, or the golden chance will pass beyond recall, and I shall go back whence I came, never more to return—never more to clasp you, dearest one, until you die too, and come to me (are you cold, that you shudder so?)—and be with me for always. Listen, listen!"

As she lifted her hand the greatest of all the great clock voices of London spoke out the midnight hour. As other voices answered from far and near Daymond shuddered, and put his dead love from him, and rose up trembling and ghastly pale.

They moved together to the window, and stood looking out. The weather was about to change; the snow was melting, the thaw drip plashed heavily from roof gutters and balconies, cornices and window ledges. As she laid her hand once more upon his shoulder the stars began to fade out one by one, and in a little while from then the eastward horizon quivered with the first faint throes of dawn.

"Wish!" she cried. "Now! now! before it is too late!" She moved as if to throw herself again upon his breast; but he thrust her from him with resolute hands that trembled no more.

"I wish," he said very distinctly, "to be Sir Robert Daymond, Baronet, and President of the —— before the year is out!"

She fell away from him, and waned, and became unsubstantial and shadowy like the ghost she was, and unlike the thing of flesh and blood she had seemed before. Nothing remained to her of lifelikeness but the scorn and anger, the anguish and reproach of her great eyes.

"Only the dead are faithful to Love—because they are dead," she said. "The living live on—and forget! They may remember sometimes to regret us—beat their breasts and call upon our names—but they shudder if we answer back across the distance; and if we should offer to come back, 'Return!' they say! 'go and lie down in the comfortable graves we have made you; there is no room for you in your old places any more!' They told me I should be sorry for coming; but I would not listen, I had such confidence. I am wiser now! Good-bye!"

A long sigh fluttered by him in the semi-obscurity, like a bird with a broken wing. There was a rattling of curtain rings, the dull sough of falling tapestry, and the opening and closing of a door. She was gone! And Daymond, waking from strangely dreamful slumbers to the cheerlessness of dying embers and burned-out candle, rang the bell for his servant, and ordered lights. A few minutes later saw him, perfectly dressed, stepping into his cab.

"Chesterfield Gardens, Mayfair," he said, giving the direction to his valet for transference to the groom.

"Beg pardon, sir, but Lady Mary Fraber's servant is still waiting!" The man pointed back to the house.

"Ah!" said Daymond, who had had a passing glimpse of alien cord gaiters reposing before his hall-fire. "Tell him I have taken the answer to his mistress myself."

And as he spoke he scattered a handful of torn-up squares of paper—the fragments of a letter—in largesse to the night and the gusty weather.

Biographical Notes

Ethna Carbery (1866-1902) was the pen name of journalist, writer, poet, and patriot Anna MacManus. She was born Anna Bella Johnston in Ballymena, Co. Antrim on 3 December 1866, and started publishing poems and short stories in Irish periodicals at the age of fifteen. She was one of the co-founders of the Daughters of Ireland, a radical nationalist women's organisation led by Maud Gonne. With the poet and writer Alice Milligan, Carbery published two nationalist periodicals, *The Northern Patriot* and *The Shan Van Vocht*, the latter considered a major contribution to the Irish literary revival. In 1901 she married poet and folklorist Séumas MacManus, though the marriage was short-lived. Carbery died at the age of thirty-five in Donegal on 2 April 1902. After her death, her husband published three volumes of her work: a book of poetry, *The Four Winds of Eirinn* (1902); and two short story collections, *The Passionate Hearts* (1903), and *In the Celtic Past* (1904).

B. M. Croker (c.1849-1920) was a popular and bestselling author who enjoyed a highly successful career from 1880 until her death forty years later. Her novels, mostly set in India, her native Ireland, and England, were witty and fast moving. Bithia Mary Sheppard was born in Co. Roscommon, the only daughter of a Church of England clergyman, and married John Stokes Croker (1844-1911), an officer in the Royal Scots Fusiliers, in 1870. The newlyweds left for Madras, India immediately after the marriage; they later lived in Bengal, and a hill-station in Wellington (where many of her stories were written). On Colonel Croker's retirement in 1892, they went to live in Co. Wicklow, and finally settled in Folkestone. She died at a nursing home in London, after a short and sudden illness, on 20 October 1920. Although Croker wrote numerous ghost stories during her career, they were only collected in 2000 as *"Number Ninety" and Other Ghost Stories.*

Clotilde Graves (1863-1932) was born in the Buttevant Barracks, Co. Cork on 3 June 1863. At the age of nine, Graves's family moved to England. She worked briefly in the British Museum while studying at the Royal Female School of Art in Bloomsbury. Often unconventional and uncompromising, Graves adopted male dress and smoked in public, both frowned upon at the time. With the intention of becoming a playwright, Graves worked as a travelling actor to learn the craft. This she did, and between 1887 and 1913 she had sixteen plays produced in London and New York. Under the pen-name "Richard Dehan", used to differentiate from her dramatic output, she also wrote historical novels as well as stories for periodicals such as *Gentlewoman*, *World*, and *Judy*. Graves retired in 1928 to a convent in Hatch End, Middlesex, where she died on 3 December 1932. Her short story collections include *The Cost of Wings* (1914), *Off Sandy Hook* (1915), *Under the Hermés* (1917), and *The Eve of Pascua* (1920).

Lady Gregory (1852-1932), noted folklorist and playwright, was born Isabella Augusta Persse to a wealthy Anglo-Irish family in Co. Galway on 15 March 1852. In 1880 she married Sir William Henry Gregory, former Member of Parliament and once-governor of Ceylon. After Sir William's death in 1892, Lady Gregory started collecting Irish legends and folklore, a lifelong interest that took form as *Cuchulain of Muirthemne* (1902), *Gods and Fighting Men* (1904), *A Book of Saints and Wonders* (1906), and *Visions and Beliefs in the West of Ireland* (1920). She was a friend and collaborator of W. B. Yeats, with whom she co-founded the Abbey Theatre in 1904. She also wrote a number of plays, mainly comedies and fantasies inspired by Irish myths. After stepping down as director of the Abbey Theatre in 1928, she retired to her family residence at Coole Park, where she did on 22 May 1932. She is today remembered as one of the leading lights of the Celtic Revival.

Beatrice Grimshaw (1870-1953) was born in Dunmurry, Co. Antrim on 3 February 1870. Though raised in the north of Ireland, and educated in France, Grimshaw is primarily associated with Australia and the South Seas, which she wrote about in her fiction and travel journalism. She was a devoted (and record-breaking) cyclist, and during the 1890s wrote for the Dublin-based magazines *Irish Cyclist* and *Social Review*. In 1904 Grimshaw was commissioned by London's *Daily Graphic* to report on the Pacific islands, around which she purportedly sailed her own cutter, never to return to Europe again. Her travel writing includes *From Fiji to the Cannibal Islands* (1907) and *In the Strange South Seas* (1908); her most popular novels are *When Red Gods Call* (1911) and *The Sorcerer's Stone* (1914); while collections such as *The Valley of Never-Come-Back* (1923) and *The Beach of Terror* (1931) feature some of her supernatural stories. After living much of her life in New Guinea, Grimshaw retired to New South Wales, where she died on 30 June 1953.

Anna Maria Hall (1800-1881), who wrote under the name Mrs. S. C. Hall, penned numerous collections, novels, and plays in which she often depicted sympathetic portraits of Ireland and its people. She was born Anna Maria Fielding in Anne Street, Dublin, on 6 January 1800. At the age of fifteen she moved to London where, in 1824, she married journalist and editor Samuel Carter Hall (1800-1889). During her career, she contributed articles, sketches, and stories to several periodicals edited by her husband, including *The Amulet* and *The Art Journal*; she also briefly edited *St. James's Magazine*. Hall is primarily remembered for her regional works, which include *Sketches of Irish Character* (1829), *Lights and Shadows of Irish Life* (1838), and *Ireland: Its Scenery and Character* (1841-43; co-written with her husband). She was also a member of the Irish temperance movement and a fervent supporter of women's rights. She died on 30 January 1881.

L. T. Meade (1844-1914) was the pen name of Elizabeth Thomasina Toulmin Smith, *née* Meade. She was born in Bandon, Co. Cork and started writing at the age of seventeen, quickly establishing herself as one of the most prolific and bestselling authors of the day. In addition to her books for young people, she also penned mystery stories, sensational fiction, romances, historical, and adventure novels; part of this tremendous output was co-written with other authors, such as Robert Eustace (1854-1943). Her most notable works include *A World of Girls* (1886), *Light o' the Morning* (1899), *The Brotherhood of the Seven Kings* (1899), and *The Sorceress of the Strand* (1903). Meade also edited *Atalanta*, a popular girls' magazine, in which she published H. Rider Haggard, R. L. Stevenson, and Katharine Tynan. She died in Oxford on 27 October 1914. Although now much of her writing is largely unread, her stories are occasionally reprinted as examples of early crime fiction.

Rosa Mulholland (1841-1921), Lady Gilbert, was born in Belfast on 19 March 1841. In 1891 she married the eminent Irish historian and archivist Sir John T. Gilbert (1829-1898). In addition to her two-volume *Life of Sir John T. Gilbert* (1905), Mulholland produced a long line of novels mostly set in rural Ireland, often drawing on local folklore, and featuring strong female characters, including *The Wicked Woods of Toberevil* (1872), *Banshee Castle* (1895), and *The O'Shaughnessy Girls* (1911). Many of her supernatural tales, originally appearing in Charles Dickens's *All the Year Round* and *Irish Monthly*, were collected in *The Haunted Organist of Hurly Burly* (1880). A further selection of her ghostly tales appears under the title *Not to Be Taken at Bed-Time & Other Strange Stories* (2013). Mulholland died at her home Villa Nova in Blackrock, Dublin, on 21 April 1921.

Charlotte Riddell (1832-1906) was born Charlotte Eliza Lawson Cowan in Carrickfergus, Co. Antrim on 30 September 1832. She moved to London in 1855 where she started her career as a writer. There, in 1857, she married engineer and inventor Hadley Riddell. By 1867 she was the editor and co-proprietor of the *St. James's Magazine* (previously edited by Anna Maria Hall). From 1857 until 1902, Riddell published more than thirty volumes, mostly novels but also short story collections. Although her realist fiction was popular during her lifetime, today she is primarily remembered for her ghost stories. She wrote five supernatural novellas, including *The Uninhabited House* (1875) and *The Haunted River* (1877), and her collection *Weird Stories* (1882) is now considered a classic of the genre. Riddell's husband died in 1881, and in 1886 she left London for nearby Middlesex. Suffering from ill health and financial difficulties, she was awarded a Society of Authors pension in 1901. Riddell died on 24 September 1906 and is buried in St. Leonard's Churchyard, Heston.

Dora Sigerson Shorter (1866-1918) was born in Clare Street, Dublin. Both of her parents were writers—her father was the noted surgeon and poet George Sigerson (1836-1925). In 1895 she married the English literary critic Clement King Shorter and relocated to London. Early in her career she contributed to magazines such as *Irish Monthly* and *Samhain*, and became friendly with the political activist Alice Furlong and the author Katharine Tynan. Shorter's volumes of poetry include *The Fairy Changeling* (1897), *Love of Ireland* (1916), and the posthumously published *Sixteen Dead Men and Other Poems of Easter Week* (1919). Shorter died in St. John's Woods, London, on 6 January 1918; Tynan later wrote that she "died of a broken heart" which she attributed to the 1916 executions. Although chiefly known for her poetry (and to a lesser extent as a sculptor) Shorter also wrote prose, including sketches collected in *The Father Confessor: Stories of Danger and Death* (1900). She is now regarded as a significant poet of the Irish Literary Revival.

Katharine Tynan (1859-1931) was born in South Richmond Street, Dublin on 23 January 1859. She was raised in Whitehall, the family home in Clondalkin. Her literary salon there attracted notables such as the mystical poet A.E. and W. B. Yeats, the latter with whom she formed a lifelong friendship. With encouragement from Rosa Mulholland, Tynan became a prolific writer, authoring more than a hundred novels in addition to memoirs, journalism, numerous volumes of poetry, and a tribute to her friend Dora Sigerson Shorter in *The Sad Years* (1918). Her works deal with nationalism, feminism, and Catholicism—Yeats declared of her early collection *Shamrocks* (1887) that "in finding her nationality, she has also found herself". Tynan died in Wimbledon, London on 2 April 1931. Her short stories, often featuring sketches of Irish life, can be found in *An Isle in the Water* (1895), *Men and Maids* (1908), and *Lovers' Meeting* (1914).

Lady Wilde (1821?-1896), born Jane Francesca Elgee in Dublin, was a poet, folklorist, nationalist, and feminist who wrote under the name "Speranza". Her earliest writings were published in *The Nation*, a pro-independence weekly newspaper; much of this nationalist poetry was collected in *Poems* (1864). She married the surgeon and writer Sir William Wilde in 1851 and had three children with him, among them Oscar Wilde. By the end of the 1860s Lady Wilde was hosting the most celebrated literary salon in Dublin at her home in Merrion Square, where Bram Stoker was a frequent guest. After her husband's death, she joined her sons in London. Based on material collected by William Wilde in the west of Ireland, Lady Wilde produced two formidable volumes: *Ancient Legends, Mystic Charms and Superstitions of Ireland* (1887) and *Ancient Cures, Charms, and Usages of Ireland* (1890). Living in relative poverty, she continued to write for magazines such as *Pall Mall Gazette*, *Tinsley's*, and *Burlington Magazine* until her death on 3 February 1896.

Acknowledgments

The editors would like to thank Mike Ashley, Reggie Chamberlain-King, James Doig, Maurice Healy, Meggan Kehrli, Alison Lyons, Ken Mackenzie, Jim Rockhill, Karen Vaughan, and Jason Zerrillo for their assistance.

❧

"The Dark Lady" by Anna Maria Hall first appeared in *The Drawing-Room Table-Book: An Annual for Christmas and the New Year* (London: Virtue, Hall & Virtue, [1847]); it was collected in *The Playfellow and Other Stories* (London: T. Nelson & Son, 1866).

"The Child's Dream" by Lady Wilde was published in *Ancient Legends, Mystic Charms and Superstitions of Ireland* (London: Ward & Downey, 1887); it also appeared in *Fairy and Folk Tales of the Irish Peasantry*, edited and selected by W. B. Yeats (London: Walter Scott, 1888).

"The Unquiet Dead" by Lady Gregory was published in *Visions and Beliefs in the West of Ireland* (London: G. P. Putnam, 1920).

"The Woman with the Hood" by L. T. Meade first appeared in the Christmas Number of the *Weekly Scotsman* (December 1897); it was collected in *A Lovely Fiend and Other Stories* (London: Digby, Long, & Co., 1908).

"The Wee Gray Woman" by Ethna Carbery was published in *The Passionate Hearts* (Dublin: M. H. Gill & Son; London: Ibister & Co., 1903).

"The Blanket Fiend" by Beatrice Grimshaw first appeared in *Liberty* (9 March 1929); it was collected in *The Beach Terror and Other Stories* (London: Cassell, 1931).

"The First Wife" by Katharine Tynan was collected in *An Isle in the Water* (London: A. & C. Black, 1895).

"Transmigration" by Dora Sigerson Shorter was collected in *The Father Confessor: Stories of Death and Danger* (London: Ward, Lock & Co., 1900).

"Not to Be Taken at Bed-Time" by Rosa Mulholland was first published in the Christmas Number of *All the Year Round* (1865); it was collected in *Not to be Taken at Bed-Time & Other Strange Stories* (Neuilly-le-Vendin: Sarob Press, 2013).

"The Red Woollen Necktie" by B. M. Croker first appeared in *Lloyd's Weekly* (16 August 1896); it was collected in *In the Kingdom of Kerry and Other Stories* (London: Chatto & Windus, 1896).

"The De Grabrooke Monument" by Charlotte Riddell first appeared in *Routledge's Every Girl's Annual 1879* (London: George Routledge & Sons); it is reprinted here for the first time.

"A Vanished Hand" by Clotilde Graves [under the pseudonym Richard Dehan] was collected in *The Cost of Wings and Other Stories* (London: William Heinemann, 1914).

About the Editors

Maria Giakaniki is an independent scholar and editor-in-chief of Ars Nocturna, a small publishing house in Athens that focuses on Gothic fiction. Her Greek translations include J. S. Le Fanu's *Carmilla* and R. L. Stevenson's *Olalla*; she has also compiled and co-translated *Gothic Tales by Victorian Women Writers* and *Gothic Tales by Modern Women Writers*, as well as edited the Greek edition of *Ghost Stories of an Antiquary* by M. R. James. She has written reviews for literary journals such as the *Irish Journal of Gothic and Horror Studies* and *The Green Book*, and delivered papers in international conferences of the Gothic.

Brian J. Showers runs Swan River Press in Dublin, Ireland. He has written short stories, articles and reviews for magazines such as *Rue Morgue*, *Ghosts & Scholars*, and *Wormwood*. His short story collection, *The Bleeding Horse*, won the Children of the Night Award in 2008. He is also the author of *Literary Walking Tours of Gothic Dublin* and *Old Albert: An Epilogue*, the co-editor of the Stoker Award-nominated *Reflections in a Glass Darkly*, and the editor of *The Green Book: Writings on Irish Gothic, Supernatural and Fantastic Literature*.

SWAN RIVER PRESS

Founded in 2003, Swan River Press is an independent publishing company, based in Dublin, Ireland, dedicated to gothic, supernatural, and fantastic literature. We specialise in limited edition hardbacks, publishing fiction from around the world with an emphasis on Ireland's contributions to the genre.

www.swanriverpress.ie

"Handsome, beautifully made volumes . . . altogether irresistible."

– Michael Dirda, *Washington Post*

"It [is] often down to small, independent, specialist presses to keep the candle of horror fiction flickering . . . "

– Darryl Jones, *Irish Times*

"Swan River Press has emerged as one of the most inspiring new presses over the past decade. Not only are the books beautifully presented and professionally produced, but they aspire consistently to high literary quality and originality, ranging from current writers of supernatural/weird fiction to rare or forgotten works by departed authors."

– Peter Bell, *Ghosts & Scholars*

NOT TO BE TAKEN AT BED-TIME
and Other Strange Stories

Rosa Mulholland

In the late-nineteenth century Rosa Mulholland (1841-1921) achieved great popularity and acclaim for her many novels, written for both an adult audience and younger readers. Several of these novels chronicled the lives of the poor, often incorporating rural Irish settings and folklore. Earlier in her career, Mulholland became one of the select band of authors employed by Charles Dickens to write stories for his popular magazine *All the Year Round*, together with Wilkie Collins, Elizabeth Gaskell, Joseph Sheridan Le Fanu, and Amelia B. Edwards.

Mulholland's best supernatural and weird short stories have been gathered together in the present collection, edited and introduced by Richard Dalby, to celebrate this gifted late Victorian "Mistress of the Macabre".

"It's a mark of a good writer that they can be immersed in the literary culture of their time and yet manage to transcend it, and Mulholland does that with the tales collected here."

– David Longhorn, *Supernatural Tales*

THE DEATH SPANCEL
and Others

Katharine Tynan

Katharine Tynan is not a name immediately associated with the supernatural. However, like many other writers of the early twentieth century, she made numerous forays into literature of the ghostly and macabre, and throughout her career produced verse and prose that conveys a remarkable variety of eerie themes, moods, and narrative forms. From her early, elegiac stories, inspired by legends from the West of Ireland, to pulpier efforts featuring grave-robbers and ravenous rats, Tynan displays an eye for weird detail, compelling atmosphere, and a talent for rendering a broad palette of uncanny effects. *The Death Spancel and Others* is the first collection to showcase Tynan's tales of supernatural events, prophecies, curses, apparitions, and a pervasive sense of the ghastly.

"Of remarkably high literary quality . . . a great collection recommended to any good fiction lover."

– Mario Guslandi

"Tynan's fiction is of a high standard, crafted in relatively simple yet still lyrical prose . . . a very assured craftswoman of the supernatural tale."

– Supernatural Tales

"Lovers of late Victorian and Edwardian ghost fiction will assuredly adore the restrained literary quality . . ."

– The Pan Review

"NUMBER NINETY"
& Other Ghost Stories

B. M. Croker

The bestselling Irish author B. M. Croker enjoyed a highly successful literary career from 1880 until her death forty years later. Her novels were witty and fast moving, set mostly in India and her native Ireland. Titles such as *Proper Pride* (1882) and *Diana Barrington* (1888) found popularity for their mix of romantic drama and Anglo-Indian military life. And, like many late-Victorian authors, Croker also wrote ghost stories for magazines and Christmas annuals. From the colonial nightmares such as "The Dâk Bungalow at Dakor" and "The North Verandah" to the more familiar streets of haunted London in "Number Ninety", this collection showcases fifteen of B. M. Croker's most effective supernatural tales.

"This is a solid collection of stories that deserve to be better known . . . they are all enjoyable ghostly tales, and ideal reading for the long winter nights."

– Supernatural Tales

"[Croker's] Indian stories evoke colonial life vividly . . . What makes them all readable are the well-observed characters and settings"

– Wormwood

www.ingramcontent.com/pod-product-compliance
Lightning Source LLC
Chambersburg PA
CBHW021140190726
48288CB00008B/2752